The Green Eyes

The Green Eyes and Other Stories

by
Henri de Saint-Georges

Translated, annotated and introduced by
Brian Stableford

A Black Coat Press Book

ISBN 978-1-61227-651-9. First Printing. July 2017. Published by Black Coat Press, an imprint of Hollywood Comics.com, LLC, P.O. Box 17270, Encino, CA 91416. All rights reserved.

TABLE OF CONTENTS

Introduction

Les Yeux verts, histoire fantastique, signed H. de Saint-Georges, here translated as "The Green Eyes," was initially published as a feuilleton in *Le Figaro* between 15 July and 8 August 1872 (skipping the issues of 1, 6 and 7 August), and was swiftly reprinted by the press associated with the newspaper in a large format, before being reprinted again in a conventional octavo format by E. Dentu the following year. The three short stories accompanying the novel in the present volume were originally published in Paris by Amyot as *Les Nuits terribles*, here translated as *The Terrible Nights*, in 1821 in a volume signed M. Henry de St.-G******, which was reprinted the following year.

Jules-Henri Vernoy de Saint-Georges (1799-1875) became famous as a prolific librettist and playwright, mostly specializing in *opéra comique* and vaudevilles, although he also wrote a considerable number of melodramas and comedies. He became manager of The Théâtre de l'Opéra-Comique in 1829 and did much of his early work for that theater, often in collaboration with other librettists and working with numerous composers—most frequently Jacques-Fromental Halévy and Adolphe Adam—but his work in other genres was staged by a wide variety of other theaters. His prose fiction was much sparser; *Les Nuits terribles* and *Les Yeux verts* effectively bracketed the rest of his career, but his most substantial items of prose fiction were the three-volume historical melodrama *L'Espion du grand monde* [The High-Society Spy] (1850)—which was subsequently adapted for the stage as a 1856 five-act drama written in collaboration with Théodore Anne for the Théâtre de l'Ambigu-Comique—and *Les Princes de Maquenoise* (1860).

Les Nuits terribles was published two years before the production of Saint-Georges' first vaudeville, *Saint-Louis, ou Les Deux diners* (1823), written in collaboration with Alexander Tardif, but it is in a very similar spirit, the three stories therein being, in effect, parodies of popular melodrama transposed into rather feverish prose. Because popular melodrama was already so wildly exaggerated, it was rather difficult to parody, there being little scope of further satirical exaggeration, but the three stories certainly make a sterling effort to do so, ramping up both the lewd elements and the horrific elements of the genre in strident fashion. The resultant plots have something in common with the genre of *contes cruels* that was pioneered shortly thereafter by S. Henry Berthoud and Petrus Borel, but their excessive comedic flamboyance distances them from the characteristic laconism and earnest intensity of the early examples of that genre.

The work that in which Saint-Georges had a hand that remains most famous today is the ballet *Giselle* (1841), for which he lent Théophile Gautier the assistance of his expertise in scripting the story, but his contribution was peripheral. It is probable that many of the other collaborative works for which he claimed a credit were originally written by his collaborators and then supplemented by his amendments when they went into production under his aegis. His most successful early works included the comic operas *L'Éclair* [The Lightning-Flash] (1935), written with Eugène Planard, with music by Halévy; *La Fille du régiment* (1840; tr. as *The*

Daughter of the Regiment), written with Jean-François Bayard, with music by Gaetano Donizetti; and *Zanetta, ou Il ne faut pas jouer avec le feu* (1840; tr. as *Zanetta*), written with Eugène Scribe, with music by Daniel Auber.

In the latter half of his long career, Saint-Georges began to write for the Opéra as well as his own theater; his work for that more prestigious stage included the five-act operas *Le Juif errant* [The Wandering Jew] (1852), written with Scribe, with music by Halévy; and *La Magicienne* (1858; tr. as *The Enchantress*), again with music by Halévy. His final work for the Opéra-Comique, and the only work he did for the stage after the publication of *Les Yeux verts*, was the three-act comic opera *Le Florentin* [The Florentine] (1874), with music by Charles Lenepveu.

Many of the librettos in which Saint-Georges had a hand during the latter half of his career, reflecting the fashions of the day, had fantastic subject-matter, so it is not entirely surprising that his final prose work should be subtitled "a fantastic story," but *Les Yeux verts* lacks the casual flamboyance of most of his work in a supernatural vein, and is carefully ambiguous in its presentation of the narrator's account of his adventure, always leaving open the possibility that the strange circumstances are the results of obsessive delusion and hallucination. That ambiguity remains even if the denouement provided by the epilogue is accepted, and the ambiguity of the epilogue itself is reinforced by circumstances that are probably best elaborated *in situ*, in the footnote that I have appended to the text immediately prior to it.

Although its tone is markedly different from that of the stories in *Les Nuits terribles* and the author's dramatic works, *Les Yeux verts* is certainly not short of melodramatic incident and abrupt plot-twists. Saint-Georges was often accused of being over-reliant in his plotting on highly improbable coincidences, and *Les Yeux verts* would certainly not have helped to modify that reputation. The stories in *Les Nuits terribles*, however, make it perfectly clear that his employment of coincidence was not a mere failure of imagination, but a deliberate contrivance; indeed, he would sometimes go to such extreme lengths to construct and orchestrate a coincidence that the relevant narrative architecture takes on a curious artistry of its own, of which Saint-Georges was surely one of the masters.

If it is considered in that light, then *Les Yeux verts* becomes something more than an implausible story, and can be seen as a deliberate and teasing exercise in implausibility, in which the possible unreliability of the narrator's testimony becomes one feature among several supporting the climactic narrative move. In spite of the difference in tone and the fifty-year gap separating the novel from the three short stories, what they have in common is perhaps more interesting than what differentiates them, and the mordant wit of the author's little commentary essays hardly seems to have altered throughout that time, save for a careful prudishness in the later work, doubtless more appropriate to a writer in his jaded seventies than one in his exuberant twenties. The juxtaposition is, in any case, interesting.

Saint-Georges was an unashamedly popular writer who always wanted to appeal to a wide audience and flatter its tastes, which he often did by sending up more pretentious works. He was regarded in his own day as a consummate craftsman rather than a considerable artist, but that judgment is a trifle unfair to the whole range of his ambition and ability. It seems probable that writing a feuilleton for *Le Figaro* was something of a *jeu d'esprit* on his part, an experiment of sorts, and that his choice of subject-matter and style were also experiments, undertaken primarily in a spirit of dabbling. Even so, and doubtless partly because of that, *Les Yeux verts* has a casual verve that sets it apart from other contemporary exercises in the same subgenre.

If, given the essential playfulness of the exercise, the novel seems a trifle shocking in its abrupt climax, it is worth remembering that it was written in the aftermath of the Franco-Prussian War, the Siege of Paris, and the brutal suppression of the Commune, when the city in which it is set and published was still reeling somewhat from its near-destruction and the traumatization of its civilian population. Its violence and horror are, at least to some extent, reflections of the mood of its time, just as the violence and horror of *Les Nuits terribles* are partly reflective of the dire legacy of the Napoleonic Wars and the instability of the Restoration that followed the emperor's final downfall. The resultant combination of attributes has helped to maintain the readability of all the texts included in the present volume, in an age where horror-comedy is a prolific and much appreciated genre.

The translation of *Les Yeux verts* was made from the copy of the 1872 edition reproduced on the Bibliothèque Nationale's *gallica* website, although the relevant copies of *Le Figaro* reproduced on the same website and the Google Books copy of the 1873 edition were also consulted for comparative purposes. The translation of *Les Nuits terribles* was made from the copy of the 1822 Amyot edition similarly reproduced on *gallica*.

Brian Stableford

THE GREEN EYES

I. Freyschutz

I had an uncle. That uncle had a cat.

My uncle adored his cat, and only loved his nephew moderately.

My uncle enjoyed an income of thirty thousand livres and seventy years. The nephew only possessed his seventeen springs.

As for the cat; it had attained the most extreme old age for cats, over twelve years. It was the Methuselah off tomcats.

My uncle called himself the Chevalier de Saint-Harem. He was a Knight of Malta, which inflicted celibacy on him in perpetuity.

This is his description: medium height, aquiline nose, the complexion of a mummy; thin lips and thick eyebrows.

But the eyes! Oh, eyes such as you have never seen, and I hope never to see again.

Those eyes were green, but a bright, ardent green for which I can find no better comparison than one of those pharmacist's bottles containing a clear emerald-colored liquid to which a gas-jet gives the appearance of a great luminous scarab, but of which the real objective is perhaps only to dazzle pedestrians in the midst of the shadows and cause a host of accidents and fractures very profitable to the learned fraternity of Monsieur Purgon's colleagues.

I recall that, while I was still very young, when my uncle fixed his gaze like a steel blade upon me, I experienced pain in my heart and stomach, similar to those caused by a stormy sea during a bad crossing.

My uncle was the calmest of men for six months of the year, an epoch blessed by me, his nephew, and by Junon, his old cook, when gout quit the Chevalier's toenails in order to go lodge in those of his friends and acquaintances.

Thus, six months of peace and six months of storms, tempests, rages and blasphemies, which had won him the reputation of a true agent of Hell—and never was any reputation better deserved.

Even his physician, an enraged philosopher thoroughly stuffed with the axioms and Messieurs Laharpe, Diderot, Helvetius and Voltaire, plugged his ears when my uncle, in the middle of one of his fits, reeled off what Junon and I called the Devil's chaplet.

My uncle then summoned one of his two favorite authors, Albertus Magnus and Paracelsus. He went to sleep regularly over the chapter entitled "Commentaries of Pythagoras on the Transmutation of Souls." What purpose would it have served to reread it, anyway, since he had known it by heart for twenty years?

The doctrines of the old Greek were his own; he preached them at every opportunity, and believed them with a faith worthy of a better objective. His convictions were such, and he supported them with such singular examples, that they had ended up attaining my young brain and poor Junon's old head.

One of the consequences of the Pythagorean religion, in my uncle, was a profound sympathy for all species of animals, whatever they were, from the most innocent to the deadliest, the bodies of those interesting creatures sooner or later, according to him, having the honor of offering us hospitality after our decease in this world.

My uncle would not have killed a flea; and when he excited the voracity of one of those accursed little vampires, he contented himself with opening his window and confiding his enemy to the winds, which took charge of finding it another destination.

In consequence of his veneration for all the animals in creation, my uncle only ate cereals, vegetables and fruits. As that cenobitic diet is extremely favorable to gout, my uncle's physician approved of it strongly, but imagine what a seventeen-year-old stomach must suffer from such an abstinence! So, the days of vacation from school were fatal days for me.

Thus, I did everything in my power to put off those days, and, with the aid of my idleness, I easily swallowed the shame of being incessantly in detention, and delighted in the slightly thin broth of the boarding-school on thinking about the spinach, cucumber and salsify of my uncle the Chevalier.

One day, however, one day of vacation—a day of joy for all schoolboys and fasting for me—old Junon, who had raised me and saw me wasting away by the week, put me in communication with a magnificent veal cutlet, to which I paid such assiduous court that in a matter of minutes I had arrived at gnawing the bone of my good fortune voluptuously.

Then a long, thin hand, seizing the last debris of my pittance, snatched it away from me violently, and the Chevalier's nasal voice made me hear the terrible words:

"Wretch! You're not thinking, then, that you might one day become a calf yourself!"

All the superstitions with which my uncle had cradled my infancy came back to my memory: one horrible story above all, which the Chevalier had told me one evening in his large drawing room, illuminated by two candles covered with a somber lampshade, in which he remembered perfectly being *the fattened ox of 1789*. And he shivered with terror as he enumerated its tortures.

Extracted from its lush pasturage in Normandy, it was taken in triumph to Paris. There, well-nourished and pampered, it was crowned with roses and green vine-branches, and then paraded through the midst of an immense crowd that uttered cries of joy and admiration at the sight of it. But having returned to its warm cowshed it heard one evening, with the marvelous perception of transmuted souls, the following dialogue between two savages of its cortege, apprentice butchers by profession:

"'You're lucky, Pierrot; it's you the inspector has charged with delivering the hammer-blow to the animal. That'll be with four six-livre coins, at least.

"'Don't complain Jérémie, you'll have the chance to bleed it; but don't make any mistake. Look, he said, approaching me and touching my huge breast, 'it's there, not an inch more or less.'

"At that moment," the Chevalier continued, "I understood everything. I understood everything, and uttered such a bellow that my two terrified torturers fell down in my litter.

"'One might think he'd understood,' exclaimed Pierrot.

"'Oh, that's beasts for you; they have presentiments, like humans,' replied Jérémie.

"The following day, a further parade: the last, alas!

"Then commenced the frightful anguish of the condemned.

"Firstly, my manger wasn't filled.

"'Don't give him anything this evening,' the inspector had said, passing by. 'The flesh is better when the belly in empty.'

"Then came the preparations for the torture: my beautiful gilded horns, treacherously attached; my poor legs fettered with solid iron rings; the sinister entry of the sacrificers; the heavy sledgehammer circling over my head.

"Then, a terrible blow, an enormous, unprecedented pain that I can still feel when I think about it...

"Finally, my fall on to the slab, and the most frightful of all the sufferings, the large knife of the operator penetrating my breast; and my blood spurting all the way to the ignoble face of my executioner..."

At that last detail of my uncle's story, I remember that I fainted. And all of that came back to mind, when my uncle pronounced those stupefying words:

"Wretch! You're not thinking, then, that you might one day become a calf yourself!"

On the evening of that day, I was taken back to school. It took more than a month for me to decide to consume my meager ration of beef, and I only did so with violent remorse, telling myself that if I had been born sooner, I might have been able to eat my uncle.

A few more words about an important character in this story: the Chevalier's cat, which I identified to you at the beginning of this chapter.

He was big, fat and black, and bore the name Freyschutz.

My uncle had baptized him thus in memory of an old German ballad on which a celebrated opera has been based.[1]

The cat was the most detestable animal one could ever see: wheedling with its master alone, treacherous, thieving, cruel, voracious, lustful and libertine; it was not lacking a single vice, and as the Chevalier accorded it a limitless impunity, there was no nasty trick that it did not play on old Junon and me. It lacerated my underwear, drank my breakfast milk, ripped up my school exercise books, turned our old maidservant's kitchen upside-down, pitilessly scratched all those its claws cloud reach and only spared the mice in the house, to the great joy of my uncle, all of whose provisions they nibbled day and night.

As for Junon, who did not possess any of the attractions of the proud goddess, her patron, she was a poor black woman brought back from the colonies many years before by Monsieur de Saint-Harem.

Junon had never known love, but she experienced, in revenge, all the furies of hate: a muted, profound, ferocious hatred that would have led her to crime if the terror that her master caused her had not restrained her in her vengeance.

She would have committed a felicide, for the object of her hatred was the damned Freyschutz. She would

---

[1] *Der Freischütz* (1821) by Carl Maria von Weber, with a libretto by Friedrich Kind, a famous product of German Romanticism featuring a Faustian bargain with the diabolical "Black Huntsman;" the "Wolf's Glen" scene in which the bargain is made had the reputation for many years of being the most gruesome known expression of music. A French version was organized by Hector Berlioz for the Paris Opéra in 1841.

have poisoned it, thrown it from the sixth floor, boiled it alive in her saucepan and served it in a fricassee to her master, as the Sire de Vergy served the heart of Gabrielle to her lover,[2] if, firstly, the Chevalier had eaten fricassees, and secondly if she had had the courage to commit the sin. For not everyone can be a murderer; that fine profession demands a certain aplomb, with which not all human creatures are endowed, fortunately for the well-being and security of their fellows.

Now, all our characters having been introduced, prepared and conscientiously exhibited, I shall begin telling this strange story.

---

[2] In Dormont de Belloy's tragedy *Gabrielle de Vergy* (1777), based on a Medieval legend; it was adapted into several operas, including one by Donizetti not produced during his lifetime but reconstituted posthumously.

II. The Death of Freyschutz

Three years had gone by.

My uncle, rendered increasingly taciturn by gout, old age and Pythagorean ideas, had felt the need to separate himself from me. My youth inconvenienced him. My innocent and joyful laughter, which he sometimes heard from his room, when I was teasing Junon or playing some prank on Freyschutz, aggravated Monsieur de Saint-Harem's nerves

I was, therefore, placed with Maître Bridaine, an advocate in the lower court, of 104 Rue de la Harpe, and I accumulated the two honorable professions of junior clerk and law student. I was nourished, lodged, heated and lighted at Maître Bridaine's expense.

This is how:

Lodgings: Poorly-furnished room on the sixth floor.

Nourishment: dry bread for breakfast; water at discretion.

Dinner: on account...or very nearly.

Heating: by the sun's rays in summer, by the flues of neighboring chimneys in winter—but as there were no neighbors, my fingertips were perpetually numb with cold in that blissful season.

Every Sunday I went go and fast with my uncle, who gave me a regular allowance of five francs a week.

Those five francs literally saved my life, for they served to procure me an indispensable supplement to the Pantagruelian meals of the honorable advocate of the lower court.

One day, however, my employer's doorkeeper, entered in Maître Bridaine's budget for the sum of eighteen francs fifty centimes per month, confessed to me that she did not have a sou to buy broth for her sick daughter. I took my weekly allowance out of my pocket and gave it to her.

I spent that week on the raft of the *Medusa*.

Thus, I had a violent appetite when I returned the following week to Monsieur de Saint-Harem's. And, while blessing Parmentier for his marvelous discovery, I devoured almost entirely by myself the enormous plate of the tuber that has classed the worthy savant among the benefactors of humankind.[3]

"Marvelous!" my uncle said. "That's what you need: vegetables, my friend, are healthy and refreshing. And then," he added, suddenly becoming somber, "if you're to be called someday to nourish yourself, in the form that destiny has given you, it will be a fully-acquired habit.

"Freyschutz, alas, must have been a celebrated gourmand in his previous existence, for he disdains his excellent milk soup for fine morsels from the neighborhood kitchens, and if he succeeds in stealing some fat poultry, you'll observe that it's always the wing to which he gives preference."

"So," I hazarded to say, "our souls only ever have as a refuge the bodies of mewling barking, ruminating, crawling, bleating, roaring, galloping animals, and the others of creation? Do they never find more noble domiciles, envelopes more comfortable and worthier of them?"

---

[3] Antoine-August Parmentier (1737-1813) became famous as the man who popularized the planting of potatoes in France as a staple crop at the end of the 18th century.

"A superior power presides over their destinies," the Chevalier replied, "but generally, the new life we enjoy is in inverse relation to the one we have quit. One can be reborn alternately slave or king, black or white; one can have the beauty of Adonis or the hump of Aesop; one very often changes sex.

"Xipharis, the sage Xipharis renowned for his virtues, Pythagoras—who knew him—tells us, subsequently became a celebrated courtesan, and counted as many lovers as they were pearls in her necklace.

"In that regard," my uncle continued, "listen to the astonishing story of the Nabob and the bayadere..."

At that moment, I uttered a cry of fright; I had just felt a sharp claw digging into what ought to have been the fleshy part of my leg, although my uncle's cuisine had long since put it in good order. Nevertheless, the pain was so sharp that I got up from the table precipitately, and I saw Freyschutz fleeing through the ground floor window, while I went back to my little rom.

My uncle, annoyed by having been so abruptly interrupted, went back to his own room—which meant, my dear readers, that neither you nor I will ever know the astonishing story of the Nabob and the bayadere.

A terrible drama took place that same evening in peaceful household of the Chevalier de Saint-Harem.

I had just gone back into the modest room, or rather mansard—I was avowed to mansards—of which, in spite of my exile, my uncle had left me the enjoyment. It was there that I shut myself away for a part of my days of leave.

I evoked in my solitude the short moments of happiness that I had enjoyed in my infancy. My mother was still alive then—the only creature that had loved me on earth. I was orphaned at the age of eight, but the memory of the person I cherished was ineffaceable for my heart. I was surrounded in my little room by objects that I had inherited from her, poor and holy relics for my filial piety: a little rosewood chiffonier next to which she worked; her portrait painted by Boily, a painter of the first empire whose pitiless brush never gave any mercy to the imperfections of his models: a red nose remained red, little eyes were not magnified.[4]

It was Boily who replied one day to a client, imploring a few strands of hair that nature had refused him: "Very well, I understand, and will give Monsieur a wig." But he had the gift of resemblance, and, thanks to him, I rediscovered my mother, with her gaze full of benevolence, her indulgent smile and the attractive charm that rendered her dear to everyone who knew her.

Worthy Boily, how many times I have blessed you in contemplating your work!

One of my treasures, the one of which I was fondest, was a ravishing Sèvres porcelain cup, my mother's favorite cup, the one in which she was offered pectoral beverages during her last illness. Her trembling hand often took it from my infantile hand. That was a proof of confidence that the poor invalid gave me, of which I was very proud and very glad.

I would not have been separated from that precious cup at the price of my blood. I only looked at it with a holy respect, and my eyes moistened with tears on thinking about the dear lips that had touched it.

Dusk was falling as I got ready to quit my redoubt in order to return to the home of Maître Bridaine, my employer.

---

[4] Louis-Léopold Boily, or Boilly (1761-1845), a prolific painter of portraits, famous for his depictions of bourgeois life.

A storm was in muted preparation; thunder was rumbling in the distance, large raindrops were beginning to batter the roof of my mansard, and I thought sadly of the immersion that threatened my own coat in the long journey from the Place Royale to the summit of the Rue de la Harpe, where I lived.

Just as I was about to close my small skylight, a violent impact struck me full in the chest, and I was almost knocked over backwards, dazed and stunned by that sudden commotion.

I did not have to search for the cause for long. Freyschutz was sitting in the middle of my room, and seemed to be laughing in his malevolent feline fashion as he contemplated my misadventure and my bewilderment.

The sharp and recent memory of his claw-thrust, combined with his new crime against my person, caused me such anger that, seizing my walking stick, I ran at my enemy, determined to administer a vigorous correction to him.

Divining the punishment that awaited him, Freyschutz launched himself on to my table, from there to my bed and then on to the little rosewood chiffonier, upsetting everything in his vertiginous course.

Finally seeking a refuge on my shelves, where I had place my cherished trinkets and my most beloved treasure, my mother's cup, he precipitated it on to the floor-tiles of my room, where I saw it shatter.

My anger became rage; distraught and beside myself, I bounded upon my enemy, and at the moment he touched the ground I launched such a violent kick at him that the poor animal turned over twice, uttered a plaintive mewl, and went to fall at the extremity of my room, where he remained, inanimate.

At that moment I perceived my uncle on the threshold of the doorway.

Pale and trembling, his terrible green eyes launched such flashes of fury at me that I was frightened.

He ran to Freyschutz, seized him in his arms, hugged him to his bosom, dissolved in tears, and vanished.

At the sight of that dolorous spectacle, a cold sweat inundated my brow.

I remained petrified by terror for a few seconds; then I left the room and went rapidly down the stairs, shouting for help and calling Junon.

"My uncle's up there and he's had a bad turn," I cried.

"Bah! Why?"

"Freyschutz is dead, and it's me who killed him."

"Bounty of Heaven!" said Junon. "You've struck a fine blow there! But no matter—the wretched cat only got what it deserves."

I confess that, at that moment, Junon's words appeared to me barbaric; I still had before my eyes the brief and dolorous death-throes of my victim, the chagrin of my uncle, whom I had deprived of his greatest affection, the tears that he had just shed, and the dangerous shock that he owed to my brutality.

For a moment, I wanted to go back upstairs, throw myself at his feet and implore my forgiveness, but I recalled the gaze full of hatred that he had launched at me. My heart failed, my courage was wanting, and I ran out of the house, distraught, almost mad, stuffed with remorse, marching at random, bumping into all those whose ill fortune placed them in my path, and no longer having any thought in my head but one: to flee as quickly as possible from a house where I had left death and despair.

Night had fallen, the storm was growling with all its force, the thunder rolling without interruption. Pale lightning-flashes blanched the flagstones of the sidewalk at intervals, and then everything fell back into complete obscurity. A torrential rain turned the gutters into muddy lakes.

In the midst of that frightful cataclysm, bare-headed, my poor garments streaming with glacial water, nothing stopped me, and, like the Jew Ahasuerus, pursued by the sword of the exterminating angel, I continued walking.

Fatigue and cold ended up appeasing somewhat the kind of delirium that had taken possession of me. I stopped, trying to recognize the place where I was.

The Seine was flowing at my feet; a somber vault hung over my head. The vault was that of the Arche-Marion.[5] How and by what route had I arrived there? That was an eternal mystery to which I never paid any heed.

I reflected then…or rather, I remembered.

It seemed to me that I emerged from a long slumber and as, at the moment of awakening, the sad events that are overwhelming us always prevent themselves to our mind with a cruel clairvoyance, my misfortunes and their consequences appeared to me all at once, rapidly and violently, as if they had been waiting for the door of

---

[5] The Arche-Marion was a superstructure that once overhung a side-street of that name in the vicinity of the modern Rue des Bourdonnais, Marion being supposedly the name of the one-time keeper of a bath-house there. It collapsed in the mid-19th century.

dreams to close in order to come and bring me their bleak realities.

I saw myself banished forever from my uncle's presence.

My employer, of whom the Chevalier de Saint-Harem was a client, would certainly not keep me in his establishment, for fear of displeasing him, and I was about to find myself devoid of money, devoid of shelter, and deprived even of Maître Bridaine's modest daily fare, henceforth the sole resource of my juvenile appetite. A violent despair seized me.

The Seine was there, bathing my aching feet; the somber murmur of the waves seemed to be calling me.

An instant of resolution, and my chagrins, my anxieties, my unhappy days and my imminent poverty would all be engulfed with me.

I took a step toward the gulf. I was about to hurl myself into it, when a dolorous moan struck my ear, and then a second, more heart-rending than the first.

The accent of that moan had nothing human about it, but it was imprinted by such suffering, and such a poignant terror, that I felt the birth of a violent desire to go to the aid of the creature, whatever it was, that was soliciting a savior.

My ears pricked, I tried to divine where the plaintive sounds had come from. With my eyes fixed on the surface of the water, then mirroring a pale moonlight, I tried in vain to discover the individual whose cries of distress had reached me.

Then, a few brasses from the bank, a head that seemed monstrous suddenly appeared. Only the head was above the surface of the water, and I was perhaps about to distinguish the creature to which it belonged when the sudden veiling of the moon enveloped the river

in a profound obscurity, and everything disappeared
from sight.

III. A Resurrection

I remained prey to a sharp anxiety for a few seconds, but the clouds dissipated, a pale light played over the waters…and the being, which the disturbance of my mind had prevented me from recognizing, appeared to me then in its natural form. I almost smiled at all the fantastic quality with which my imagination had surrounded it.

It was simply an enormous barbet dog, exhausting itself in vain efforts to get back to dry land, which a deviation of the current had brought close to the bank. And I, who wanted to destroy myself, to whom the river had seemed to be the sole resource for my woes, felt full of compassion for the poor animal that was fighting for its life in the waves into which I was ready to hurl myself.

I leapt into a punt moored to the bank. I detached the chain that retained it there and, seizing the gaffe destined to push the frail boat away from the shore, I reached the open water in the direction from which the barbet was coming toward me.

Lightning flashed in the sky, and in that sudden clarity, I was able to distinguish the unfortunate animal a few brasses from the punt. I held out the gaffe to it, to which it clung with the instinct of self-preservation that all beings in danger share.

I drew it toward me, seized it by a thick collar that it was wearing, and succeeded with a painful effort in getting it into the punt, which I brought back to the shore.

"Oh, so it's you, Monsieur river-prowler, who takes excursions in our punts without their master's permission," said a sort of colossus, advancing toward me, a mariner of the port, whom the boat doubtless served for the transport and loading of coal aboard ships.

"Excuse me," I replied, showing him my half-drowned passenger. "I couldn't resist the desire to snatch this poor beast from death, which was heading straight for the nets at Saint-Cloud."

"They don't give medals for that," said the colossus, "but that's all right, it's good, what you did, and I forgive you. Saving a dog is sometimes better than saving a man. Well," he continued, "it's necessary to make him cough up the excess he's drunk, or you'll see him blow up like a whale and burst like a fly."

While speaking, he seized the enormous dog by the tail and held him head-down for a few moments, until he had expelled by the mouth and the nostrils everything that he had absorbed in his perilous journey.

"There, that's done it. Let's lay him on the sand now and pour a few drops of this old grain alcohol into his throat; that'd bring back a dead man, and this fellow's only half-dead."

And he handed me the flask, of which I made the usage that he indicated.

The barbet pricked up its ears, uttered a dull yap of wellbeing, shook off the water that was dampening its thick coat, made an effort to stand up, and fell back heavily.

But the courageous animal renewed its attempt. This time it remained upright, came to press itself against me, as if it were in search of a refuge, looked at me for a few seconds with its large blinking eyes, and licked my hand.

"Poor beast," I said, very moved, forgetting the mariner, who was listening to me. "You give yourself to me, I take you—but how can I keep you alive when I don't have the means to live myself, when I was about to throw myself in the river from which I pulled you out?"

"Aha!" exclaimed the port worker. "Well, that's a fine thing! What, my lad, you were about to serve a platter to the fish of the Seine? Come on, you're young, you appear to me to be strong and well-built, what the devil's got into you? Poverty, despair—you're out of work. That's it, isn't it?"

Nonplussed by having thus revealed my sad secret before the man, a nod of the head was my only response to his question.

"Well, that's stupid, and it's bad," he continued. "It's only cowards who can't support misfortune. Come on, my lad, courage; you have a good heart, otherwise you wouldn't have saved that poor animal. A good heart—that always gives me confidence, personally. Here," he said, taking an old leather purse out of his pea-jacket, "my last fortnight's pay is in there. That'll get you out of trouble, at least for the present; the good God will do the rest.

"Oh, take it," he added, seeing me refuse the purse he was holding out. "We're at ease, thank God, my old wife and me. If you want to give it back to me some day, ask in the port for Père Bonnefoi, stevedore. Any of the comrades will tell you my address."

And, dropping the purse at my feet, be started running along the strand, and soon disappeared in the midst of the obscurity that the dark clouds had brought back.

I tried to follow him, but the fatigue and exhaustion caused by so much emotion had annihilated my strength. The purse was still there, without my having dared to pick it up, but a ray of hope traversed my heart.

All this is providential, I said to myself. *If I still exist, it's because Heaven wanted it. The money that brave worker offered me so nobly forbids me henceforth to take my life, and I have to live to be worthy of his generosity. Besides which, as he said to me, killing oneself is cowardice. Let's try, then, the terrible combat of perseverance and energy against misfortune. So many people have sustained that unequal struggle; why shouldn't I be victorious? Why shouldn't I find within me the arms that a sound education has given me, which the woes and privations of my youth will render stronger and surer?*

That generous resolution reanimated me spontaneously. I quit the boundary-marker on which lassitude had constrained me to sit down, and picked up the mariner's purse

Alms, I said to myself. *Well, so be it; it's so noble and so touching that I needn't blush at it.*

I was about to go away and try to find my way again when the barbet, which had never taken its eyes off me, grabbed the tail of my coat and uttered a dolorous howl.

"Come on, come on, my poor companion," I exclaimed, caressing it. "I won't abandon you."

And it followed me all the way to the Rue de la Harpe, leaping and capering around me.

After many detours, and with some difficulty, I got back to Maître Bridaine's house, and my modest lodgings. I went to throw myself on my hard bed. The barbet, collapsing with fatigue, went to sleep in a corner.

"Poor animal," I said, looking at it, "the cold floor of my room is a hard bed for you, but it's still better than the one from which I extracted you."

I soon became drowsy, and I had a horrible nightmare.

It seemed to me that an enormous mass was weighing upon my chest. I made prodigious but futile efforts to reject it.

Suddenly, I felt a frightful bite on my right cheek. I uttered a cry of pain, and I then perceived Freyschutz, crouched on top of me, voluptuously licking up the blood that was escaping from my wound.

The hound, upright and motionless, its two paws placed on my bed, was looking at me with compassion, and tears were falling silently from its large round eyes.

I experienced a gradual weakening during that horrible torture; life seemed to be only awaiting a few further suctions on my enemy's part to quit me, when a violent blow shook my door.

I extracted myself from my torpor and sat up on my bed.

The frightful phantom disappeared.

The nightmare vanished, and I then enjoyed the immense wellbeing that one experiences on waking up after the hallucinations of a frightful dream; but the dream had had such a character of verity, I had sensed myself stifled so painfully by the horrible feline that was oppressing me... its sharp teeth, penetrating my flesh had caused me such agony that I put my hand to my cheek to search for my wound there, simultaneously surprised and very happy not to bring it away covered in the blood by which I thought that I was covered.

Who can tell us the secrets of dreaming, its causes and its origin? Who can tell us where the abnormal state into which slumber plunges us comes from? The labors of digestion, the overexcitement of the day, or an unhealthy and nervous state? But why do the most sinister depictions sometimes present themselves when nothing has troubled either the mental or the physical state of our organism, when nothing has disturbed its equilibrium, when our conscience is tranquil, our health perfect and the joys of life surround us? Why the persistence of the same dream for several consecutive nights?

One of the most honorable men I have known regularly saw himself executed in the Place de Grève, between four and five o'clock in the morning—and that went on for three months.

Are they memories of another life, or presentiments of a life to come that sleep brings us?

Dreams have often and very stupidly been explained, from Joseph, son of Jacob, to Mademoiselle Lenormand, the Empress Joséphine's card-reader.[6] Pretended diviners have given the key to nocturnal visions; it has only served to trouble the brains of a host of old women and fatten the lottery, that discovery of the malign Casanova, who obtained greater benefits than all his disciples from that game of chance, because he wagered on the largest numbers of life: human weakness and cupidity. Fine lotteries, those, in which schemers and rogues almost always win with unbeatable hands.

My door was shaken again by the fist of my nocturnal visitor, and the quavering voice of my porter caused me to hear these words:

"A letter has come from your uncle. It's said to be urgent."

---

[6] Marie Anne Lenormand (1772-1843) became the most famous cartomancer of the era, largely by virtue of her ardent self-publicizing endeavors, which included claiming to have given her advice to the Russian Tsar as well as the French Empress, not to mention Marat and Robespierre (who presumably failed to profit from her prognostications.)

I opened the door immediately, and by the light of a smoky candle I deciphered, painfully, these lines, whose author seemed to have divined the telegraphic style:

Uncle very ill. Doctor in despair. Me much afflicted. Come very quick. Him going soon. Your servant, Junon.

That letter caused me such a violent emotion that I fell back on my bed, unable to pronounce a single word.

"Well, well, what are you doing there?" said the concierge, and added, by way of consolation: "If your uncle is as ill that, he must want to bless you before closing his eyes, the poor dear man."

IV.

I went downstairs rapidly and resumed the road to the Place Royale.

That quarter, so sad during the day, is a somber desert by night.

The low and massive arcades under which the torches of Louis XII's courtiers once shone, were scarcely illuminated then by a few sordid street-lights, the ruddy glow of which augmented the sinister aspect of the galleries. The likes of Cinq-Mars, de Thou and Marion Delorme had been replaced by a few belated citizens returning to their ancient dwellings.

I reached the Chevalier de Saint-Harem's house, situated at the back of the courtyard of an old town house.

Everything about my uncle's abode was sad: the building it occupied, the ancient tapestries that covered the walls of his apartment, the broad, cold staircase by means of which one went up to it. A few copies of Murillo, Hermosa the elder and Zurbaran, representing lugubrious subjects, were hung here and there in the rooms that preceded my uncle's bedroom, and were in perfect harmony with that somber dwelling.

My heart was beating violently as I climbed the stairs that led to the Chevalier's drawing room.

Old Junon was waiting for me there.

"Shh!" she said to me, pointing at Monsieur de Saint-Harem's bedroom. "Listen!"

I heard a dull murmur then, monotonous, regular and cavernous, coming from that room.

"It's the death-rattle," the woman went on. "He's been like that for an hour. The doctor quit him, telling me that there was nothing more he could do for now, but that he'd call back at about midnight."

"And whence came this sudden illness?" I exclaimed. "What can have put the Chevalier in such a state?"

"You," Junon replied. "The grief that the death of Freyschutz caused him provoked a congestion—that, I believe, is the word the doctor used. The gout had risen to his stomach; we transported him to his bed, and it's the last night he'll spend there, I think."

"And you've left him alone?" I said to the maidservant, with a swift anger. "No one with him to soothe him, perhaps to save him?"

"Yes," said Junon, "there's someone with him."

"Who, then?"

"His damned cat," the woman replied, with a demonic laugh. "Monsieur le Chevalier didn't want to be separated from it, and they're both there, the cat on a sofa and the master in the bed."

I pushed the black woman away with a gesture of horror and disgust, and I went into my uncle's bedroom precipitately.

The room had such a funereal aspect! It was as cold and silent as a tomb.

At the back, there was a vast alcove draped with faded lampas. It was in that alcove that the Chevalier de Saint-Harem was dying.

At the moment when I approached him, the dying man's hoarse rattle suddenly stopped. He opened his eyes and recognized me; a flash of reason illuminated his pale face, but at the same time, it was painted with such an expression of wrath that I recoiled, seized by terror.

"Come, Monsieur," he said to me, in a voice strangled by the malady, "come and contemplate your work. This is where your brutality has brought me. I know that a strong mind like yours wouldn't admit that the loss of a miserable creature like this"—he showed me the cadaver of Freyschutz, placed on a chaise-longue facing is bad—"can cause such a violent shock that it could bring about the death of the man who experiences it, but I, who am only an old man, simple of heart and mind, have the good sense to attach myself to those who love me. Now, that animal loved me; he only loved me, spiteful for everyone else, good and affectionate for his master alone...

"You knew that; you knew that he was my consolation in the pains of existence, that the sight of him and his caresses brought a relief to my cruel suffering; and without any regard, without any pity for the man who was your second father, you had the cruelty of putting to death the poor creature that enabled him still to love life! Oh, that was a great weakness on my part, wasn't it? More than that, perhaps dementia. Well then, it was necessary to lock me up like a madman, not give me a shock that is killing me!"

A sudden suffocation cut off his speech; his respiration stopped and his head fell back on the pillow.

I thought that my uncle was expiring; I launched myself toward him; I took him in my arms to sustain him, but he shoved me away abruptly; his gaze suddenly recovered its frightful gleam.

"Listen," he said to me, making a painful effort. "I expect one last service from you. Open that writing-desk. Take from the middle drawer an envelope sealed in black, and bring it to me.

I obeyed the Chevalier automatically, and gave him the envelope for which he had asked me.

"Monsieur," he went on, "this is my testament. By this document I make you my sole heir. I leave you me entire fortune, my income and my property, the house I live in and an income of about thirty thousand livres."

"Oh, uncle!" I exclaimed. "So much generosity..."

"Don't hurry to thank me yet," added Monsieur de Saint-Harem, with a smile so perfidious and malevolent that it is engraved in my memory as one of the most dolorous impressions of my life. "This testament was made in an epoch when I still believed in your affection for me; I had counted that my benevolence, the education I have given you, the paternal cares that I took during your childhood, were worth a sincere and durable gratitude on your part."

"But your benevolence will be eternally present in my memory and my heart," I told him, with a vivid emotion.

"And how have you repaid that benevolence? By rejecting my convictions"—the Chevalier paled excessively as he pronounced those words—"while abridging my days by the cruel action you have just committed!

"Monsieur," he continued, becoming increasingly animated, "I do not know what will become of my soul; I do not know what new existence is reserved for it, but be certain that my hatred for you will survive, constant and unrelenting, the death to which I am about to fall prey. As for my vengeance in this world, I can at least satisfy it by destroying this testament..."

And combining action with the threat, he seized the document, which he had dropped on to his bed, and was about to tear it up when a nervous spasm separated his trembling hands.

A hoarse and heart-rending cry escaped from his breast, his eyes closed...he was dead.

My legs buckled beneath me; I articulated a few words of grief through my tears, and I fell to my knees next to the corpse of the man who had cursed me in his last hour, but with whom my only family tie disappeared, the last of those to whom nature and blood bound me.

Suddenly, I stood up. I thought I had heard—no, I *had* heard—a sigh...and, faint as it was, I was sure that I had not been mistaken.

What if he's alive, I said to myself, *what if what I took for death is only a weakening, a faint, a lethargy?*

I rang violently. Junon came running; a man followed her.

The man was the doctor, who, faithful to his word, had come to assure himself that his fatal horoscope had been realized.

"Look, look, examine him!" I exclaimed. "Perhaps there's still some hope! Perhaps my uncle's still alive!"

The doctor approached and put his hand over the Chevalier's heart.

The heart was no longer beating.

Then he took a mirror and placed it over Monsieur de Saint-Harem's lips.

The glass of the mirror was not misted.

"Your uncle is no more," he told me. "That's one honest man fewer. I had a good and generous client in him, and you've lost a relative who loved you tenderly."

He gave me his adieux and left.

"Go," I said to Junon. "I'll keep vigil tonight next to Monsieur de Saint-Harem's body."

Then I found myself alone in that sad room, faintly illuminated by a lamp placed on the mantelpiece.

I sat down in the large armchair in which the Chevalier habitually took his siesta.

That armchair was touching my uncle's bed, and I felt a shiver of terror on encountering the hand of the Chevalier, whose arm, disturbed by the doctor's expertise, was hanging over the edge.

I summoned up all my courage and replaced the arm next to the body, of which a glacial cold was beginning to take possession.

But another duty, much more painful, remained for me to fulfill. Dear friends had accomplished it for my mother; it was me who had to take charge of it with regard to my only relative. That duty, the final adieu of the living creature to the dead ne, consisted of closing the eyes, an ancient custom of which the psalmist sang, and which the Catholic rite has consecrated.

At that thought, I felt myself go pale and begin to tremble. I was about to draw the somber veils of eternity over those eyes, whose glare I had never been able to sustain.

I prayed, imploring God for the strength to accomplish that pious mission, and advanced toward the bed, stronger and more reassured. But death had already commenced its work; the dull and vitreous eyes of the Chevalier only inspired a profound pity in me.

I lowered the deceased's eyelids respectfully.

Imagine my surprise, however, on seeing those eyelids raise themselves again under my hand, as if the will of the dead man had activated them.

Twice more, my attempt had the same result; then, at the second, it seemed to me that the eyes widened considerably, that the pupils dilated, and that the Chevalier's gaze was about to pierce the opaque clouds that enveloped it.

A new fear took possession of me, and I went back swiftly to huddle in the armchair that I had quit.

Slumber, that imperious tyrant, from whose law no one can withdraw, came to put an end to so many poignant emotions...

I slept for a few minutes, or perhaps a few hours; I do not know; but when I awoke, the lamp had ceased burning and the dead man's room was in the deepest obscurity. Thick darkness surrounded me, and in the initial disturbance of awakening, I was unable at first to take account of where I was, nor of what had happened there.

Gradually, the memory returned, and with the memory, all the terrors that I had felt assailed me simultaneously.

I was suffering physically as well as mentally; I was shivering in my clothing, which was still damp, my body was icy and my head on fire; my blood was no longer circulating; the sinister silence that reigned around me was suffocating me; I lacked air.

My jerky, intermittent respiration was becoming more painful and more difficult with every passing moment.

I wanted to get out of that lugubrious apartment, but my paralyzed limbs retained me there in spite of my efforts.

Suddenly, the silence was troubled by a strange noise: a sort of scratching, like that produced by a fingernail on silk.

Then everything fell silent.

A few seconds later, the same noise recommenced, but louder and more precipitate. Seeking to pierce the shadow, I directed my gaze toward the place from which the noise was coming.

A mortal terror gripped me. I had just perceived, a few feet away from me, my uncle's terrible eyes fix on mine, and those wild and green eyes were shining at that moment with a fire so intense that I hid my head in my hands in order to escape the torture they were causing me.

A few seconds went by like that.

What has happened while I was asleep? I asked myself then. *Has life reappeared in the Chevalier? Has he been transported to some other place in his room?*

I could easily take account of the last fact. I extended my arm toward the bed on which my uncle was lying, and I felt his body, already rigid, in the place where I had seen it.

Suddenly, a frightful mewling—or rather, a tiger's roar—made itself audible on the chaise-longue where Freyschutz had been deposited.

A terrible idea occurred to me, and at that idea, a cold sweat covered my brow. My teeth chattered as if to break; a general tremor took hold of my entire being; my tongue thickened, my throat tightened, and my eyes bulged from their orbits, fixing with an invincible obstinacy on the green eyes, from which I could not tear my gaze away.

"Oh my God!" I stammered, with a profound horror. "Was my uncle right? Can his soul have rendered existence to that hideous animal?"

My legs buckled beneath me, and I fell on to the bedroom carpet.

V. The Florist

Two days after that terrible night, the funeral of the Chevalier de Saint-Harem took place.

The witnesses of that sad ceremony were not numerous; the somber and peevish character of the Chevalier had driven his former friends away a long time ago. There were, in consequence, only four of us to render the last duties to my uncle: the doctor, the native woman Juno, Maître Bridaine and me.

I confess that I was very distracted during those long hours of mourning and prayer. My thoughts were wandering elsewhere.

My uncle was not dead for me. We certainly escorted his mortal remains to the field of rest, but his soul, that divine emanation, that hearth of life, which animates matter, had perhaps only changed envelope on quitting the exhausted body that it had inhabited for seventy years. I dared not think without terror, and above all without a dolorous contraction of the heart, of the refuge that it had chosen, or had perhaps been imposed upon it.

When the ceremony was over, I did not want to return to the Chevalier's house. I did not feel that I had the strength to brave the recent memories with which it was filled; and then, it must be said, I shivered at the idea of seeing Freyschutz again and confronting the terrible gaze that had frightened me for such a long time.

I went back to my former dwelling.

A few steps from Maître Bridaine's house, a dog ran to meet me, barking joyfully.

"Oh, Monsieur!" cried my porter, on seeing me. "It caught your scent at a distance, the poor animal. For a quarter of an hour it hasn't been able to stay still, never ceasing to run from my lodge to the coaching entrance. That's a fine beast, and how he loves you!"

I felt so emotional at that evidence of affection, which was lavished upon me in the midst of my sadness and my isolation, that I seized the large head of my new friend and was getting ready to kiss it when I noticed his collar—the collar that had aided me to pull him out of the water—and I read on a little copper plate the words, almost effaced by wear: *Mademoiselle Henriette, 12 Rue Copeau.*

That's the barbet's owner, I said to myself. *How she must miss him! So many anxieties for three days; would it not be a good deed to take him back today?*

And without hesitation, I set out *en route* for number 12, Rue Copeau.

Something happened during that journey that astonished me greatly, and of which I only obtained an explanation toward the end of the day. My four-legged friend followed me at first, joyful, alert, frisky and capering, barking at all his peers, who fled at his imposing aspect. As we approached the goal of my visit, however, I perceived that he became sad and mute. Several times, he stopped, deaf to my summons.

My surprise was complete when, a few paces from the house to which I was going, he lay down next to a boundary-marker, and obstinately refused to follow me any further. Caresses, threats, everything was futile. Then he looked at me so sadly and simultaneously so resolutely, that I did not insist any further.

In fact, I thought, *perhaps the person I'm looking for no longer lives in this neighborhood, and I'll find my companion in the same place, unless he takes advantage of my absence to quit me, in which case he's nothing but one ingrate more, among so many others.*

I headed toward number 12, and found myself in front of an old, dark, poorly-constructed house, which, by virtue of a phenomenon of equilibrium common to many other habitations of that kind in our fine city of Paris, was still standing, in spite of its cracks and its dilapidation.

An old shoemaker's paltry shop communicated with the dark alley into which I went, but the artiste immediately emerged from his shop, shoe-horn in hand and shouted at me in a drunken voice: "Hey, you! Where are you going like that, without speaking to the concierge?"

"Mademoiselle Henriette," I shouted to him. "Doesn't she live here?"

"Mademoiselle Henriette doesn't receive men at home, and apart from Monsieur Mimi Taloche, no human being ever enters her domicile."

"I've brought Mademoiselle Henriette good news," I replied to the Cerberus, "and I'm sure that she'll see me."

"That's her affair, after all," the fellow said, returning to his hovel. "If she's disturbed, that's her affair."

I had only forgotten one thing in my precipitation, which was to discover the floor on which the person I wanted to see lived.

I knocked on the first door I found.

"Mademoiselle Henriette?" replied the old woman to whom I addressed myself. "Keep going up, Monsieur, as if you were going to visit Napoléon on the Colonne Vendôme, and when you can't go any further, that's it."

I had not imagined, in fact, that one could climb so high; it made my mansard in the Rue de la Harpe seem like an entresol.

On the final stage I lost my footing and had to cling on to the banister of the frightful stairway. At the noise I made in stopping my fall, and the cry of fright that I uttered, a young woman ran out on to the landing, emotional and tremulous on perceiving me.

If that scene had happened in the evening, I could have believed it an apparition.

Tall, thin and dressed in black, the unknown woman's face was so pale that she resembled a phantom rather than a living creature. And yet, it was not that strange exterior that caused me the violent surprise that I experienced; a confused, inexplicable memory gripped my heart at the sight of her, and I stood before her, motionless and nonplussed, without being able to speak to her.

"What do you want, Monsieur?" the young woman asked me, in a soft voice, so faint that I could hardly hear it.

"Mademoiselle Henriette," I relied, mastering my emotion—but the ascent I had just made had been so long and difficult that my head was spinning as I arrived at the destination of my journey.

She tried to smile, but the sketched smile was nothing more than a sort of contracted rictus that made me feel ill to see.

"I'm the person you're looking for," she added, "if you'd care to come in—but lower your head a little, for the room has the roof for a ceiling and it took me six months to get used to it."

"You've been living here for six months?" I said to her. "But there's neither air nor daylight in these lodgings!"

"There's very little," she replied, "but that little window is so close to the sky that it gives me enough light for my work."

"You're a florist, Mademoiselle," I replied, indicating a crude fir-wood table on which a magnificent artificial white rose was blossoming."

"Yes, Monsieur, but can I ask...may I know...?" she added, hesitantly.

"What brings me here...I've come to tell you that I recently had the good fortune to pull a poor dog out of the water that was drowning in the Seine..."

"Oh my God!" she cried excitedly, interrupting me. "Fidele! My poor Fidele!"

"...And on his collar," I continued, "your name and address were engraved."

"And you've saved him and you're bringing him back to me. Oh, you don't know, Monsieur, the joy you're causing me. Fidele! He's my only consolation in this world, the only thing I inherited from my poor mother. I've been weeping for him for three days. I searched the whole quarter for him in vain. He went out at dusk with...with someone who took him away, and I haven't seen him since."

"I hoped that he would follow me all the way here, but he stopped a short distance away from the house, and nothing would convince him to come in with me."

"Oh, pardon me, Monsieur, pardon me for quitting you like this, but I'll go down and call him. He'll come with me, I'll answer for that."

But as if he had heard what had just been said, the barbet hurtled into the room, ran to his mistress, rolled at her feet with a fine folly, and then came back to me, seized the tail of my coat and drew me to Mademoiselle Henriette as if to indicate his savior to her.

48

"My poor Fidele," she said, her eyes full of tears, "my only friend, here you are returned to our sad abode; you've come back to share my suffering and my misery..."

She stopped suddenly. "Monsieur," she said, in a confused voice, "excuse me for speaking like that before you; I don't complain to anyone about my sad lot, but I'm so happy at the moment that my heart couldn't hold back the confession that just escaped me."

I was about to reply when I was distracted by the barbet's bizarre maneuvers within the room. He was going back and forth, ferreting in all the corners and plunging into a obscure cabinet that I had not noticed.

"Oh, I understand why Fidele refused to follow you," said Mademoiselle Henriette, showing me the dog. "He feared that he might encounter here a person he doesn't like, who has often mistreated him badly..."

Footsteps were audible in the corridor; the barbet's anger increased, and his drawn-back lips left uncovered long sharp teeth, which seemed ready to devour the person who was approaching.

VI. Monsieur Mimi Taloche

Mademoiselle Henriette was seized by a nervous tremor that forced her to sit down, but she made such an imperious gesture to Fidele that the latter, while growling, went back to the depths of the poor redoubt.

Then, a young man of seventeen or eighteen years of age, the most hideous example I had ever seen of the Paris gamin, appeared on the threshold.

Small, thin, meager, with russet blond hair stuck in kiss-curls over his temples and a deformed cap on his head, his etiolated body was covered by a smock that had once been blue; and with that costume, an arrogant and provocative expression, a hoarse voice, blinking, gummy and malevolent eyes: that was the ugly individual who came into Mademoiselle Henriette's room.

"Well, what?" he said, addressing the young woman, designating the cupboard where Fidele, who had not stopped growling, had taken refuge. "You've replaced your beast with another, then? You always have to have an animal with you? Fetch your porter, then, he'll be good for something, this one—he'll make soup."

"The dog you mean," replied Henriette, "is our dog, it's Fidele."

"Fidele?" said the gamin. "He's come back from far away, then. I thought his carcass was at the bottom of the Seine."

"And how do you know that he fell into the water?" asked the seamstress.

"Because it's me who threw him in."

"You!" cried Henriette, horrified.

"That astonishes you because I look so frail, don't I? But Mimi isn't stupid. I have my tricks. I make melodrama like Monsieur Pixérécourt. I coaxed the animal while attaching a big stone to his neck and I pushed him into the big bathing station, where he disappeared like one of the vanishing nutmegs of Monsieur Lesprit, the conjurer in the Place du Louvre. He must have chewed through his cord, the damned barbet, to come back to the land of the living."

Mademoiselle Henriette, motionless and consternated, seemed to have lost the power of speech; her lips were moving without producing any sound, but her features expressed anger and indignation as she listened to that frightful story.

As for me, that barbaric cynicism revolted me to such a degree that, emerging from the penumbra with which the falling dusk had surrounded me, I advanced toward him and said to him: "What you've done in infamous, and you're a wretch."

"Well, well," he replied, looking at me in amazement. "Henriette has company! Well, that's a good one. Has Mademoiselle Virtue taken a lover?"

"I'm not Mademoiselle's lover; I only met her a few minutes ago; but you, whom I know even less, I judge by the unworthy action you've committed and I repeat to you that you're a wretch."

"Oh, no words, no words, bourgeois," said the gamin, striking the pose of a kick-boxer. "I can play, me, you see, I'm a student of Lachincholle, and if people annoy me, I give them a tap..."

"You won't be giving any taps!" I replied, beside myself and seizing him by the collar. "And I order you to get out of here!"

"Ha ha! He's very droll, this m'sieur, who wants to throw the master of the house out of the door."

"You're not the master of the house," the young seamstress interrupted, "you're my brother, to my misfortune; but this is my home; I receive you here out of charity, I nourish you on my work, and henceforth, I don't know you."

"Oh, God of God, Lord God, that's a lot of fuss for a dog. That dog eats like four, and we have scarcely enough for two; the great hairy mutt scoffs half our pittance. I drowned him because he was a useless mouth, that's all!"

"Let's finish this," said the young seamstress, who was beginning to recover her composure, seeing a defender close by. It's money you want, isn't it, like yesterday, like always. Here's ten francs; it's half what the mistress florist gave me for a fortnight's work. That's all I can do for you," she added, sighing, "but you must never come here again."

"That's fine, that's fine, little sister," said the gamin, pocketing the ten francs. "I'll break my lease, and snap, snap, it's finished between us. Anyway, I have an industry now; I'm a cook for the animals in the Jardin des Plantes; it's me who cuts up those messieurs' dinner. And they're fashionably-nourished gastronomes; one might think all the dead horses in Paris were fattened up for their digestive juices. So I count on filching a few slices from my clients. Your two cart-wheels will be for lodgings and luxury objects.

"Adieu, sister's lover, salutations to the company," he added, laughing, bowing to me with a snigger. "Make her happy if you can; she's a good girl, with a hand over her mouth, and it might as well be yours as another; you have a good fist, that's a capital, it'll do all right in a brawl. You don't look like a toff, it's true, but who knows? Perhaps Monseigneur is maintaining his incognito?"

And he went out whistling a tune that was running the streets in that epoch.

I had no idea of such language and such depravity, so I stood there stupefied in the middle of the room while the gamin's whistling faded away in the distance in the meanders of the stairway.

When I turned back to Mademoiselle Henriette she dissolved in tears.

"Oh, Monsieur," she said to me, amid her sobs, "hazard has brought you to a very unfortunate creature, but my greatest dolor is having such a degraded being for a brother. Both orphans, and a few years younger than him, I've cared for him and brought him up. I hoped to make an honest man of him, a good worker, but you've seen what he's become. When I thought he was in the workshop where I had him taken on, he was vagabonding in the streets of Paris, where infamous acquaintances have finished perverting him.

"One day, he was brought back to me dead drunk. He only comes back here when he can't find some ignoble abode for shelter. He takes everything from me that I earn with such difficulty. I had two sets of silver cutlery and a little gold watch; he took them during my absence and sold them. This is the only jewel I have left," she added, taking a little locket from her bosom. Its case isn't valuable, but it doesn't matter; he'd already have taken it from me if he knew about it—so I've always hidden it from him carefully, for I value this locket more than my life." She raised it tenderly to her lips as she spoke.

I darted a furtive glance at the locket.

"May I see it?" I said to the seamstress. She handed it to me. It was the portrait of a man who was still young.

Suddenly, I uttered a cry of fright; I had just recognized my uncle's green eyes.

I remained mute with surprise for a few moments. Henriette was looking at me, utterly nonplussed.

"Forgive me," I said, making an effort to collect myself. "The profound emotion that this portrait causes you has touched me all the more because it reminded me of a friend…a relative…," I added, hesitantly, "and if you will deign to inform me of the name of the man whose image you possess, you'll be rendering me a veritable service."

"Oh, Monsieur," she said, "I'd be only too glad if I knew myself, and the mystery that surrounds it will be an eternal dolor to me."

"But may I at least know from whom you obtained the locket?"

"From my mother, Monsieur, my poor mother. On the day when I had the immense dolor of losing her, she drew me close to her, clasped me to her heart and said: 'When I'm no more, take this portrait from my neck, from which I've never been parted. It's that of the man who has caused all our misfortunes, but whom I loved very much. I've always hidden his name from you, and I've sworn only to reveal it in my last hour. That hour has come…'

"She was about to continue, but the words expired on her lips. Death sealed her mouth forever."

"And what powerful interest do you attach to that revelation, then?" I asked her, unable to resist my curiosity.

"A very great interest, Monsieur," she added, dissolving in tears. "The man whose face you see was my father."

A thunderbolt striking at my feet could not have given me such a shock.

Henriette was so emotional herself that she would not have been able to respond to further questions on my part.

I stammered a few words of apology for my indiscretion, and I went away swiftly. I don't know how I managed, troubled as I was, to descend the young seamstress' two hundred steps.

Henriette, the daughter of the Chevalier de Saint-Harem, seemed to me something so strange that my reason refused to admit it.

The Chevalier in love!

Even more, a woman in love with the Chevalier—that appeared to me to be beyond all plausibility.

In was forgetting, it is true, that my uncle had not always been sixty years old; that he was said to have been handsome in his youth; that age and the obsession that absorbed him had doubtless given his gaze since then the sinister gleam that made me tremble.

It was necessary for me, at all costs, to know that story. But who could tell me, when Henriette appeared not to know it herself?

I took account then of the effect that the sight of her had produced on me. There was, in fact, between her and the Chevalier de Saint-Harem one of those family resemblances that are transmitted from father to children, and often from generation to generation.

I was walking rapidly, agitated and feverish, my eyes fixed on the paving-stones of the street, which I could not see, when I collided violently with a man coming toward me, whom I had not seen. The shock was such that would inevitably have knocked me over but for a house against which I backed, and which preserved me from a bad fall.

"Pardon me, bourgeois," said the individual whose encounter had been so rude. "That's what comes from counting the paving-stones instead of looking ahead."

Disturbed by the shock I had received, red with anger, I was getting ready to do my aggressor a bad turn when I saw before me a veritable colossus who was looking at me, smiling at my distraught face.

I took step toward him, and was about to push him away without calculating the inequality of our strength, when I suddenly seized his hand and launched myself into his arms with a veritable transport of joy.

VII. The Testament

"Well, good!" the stranger said to me, bewildered. "You have no rancor. I was expecting a solid punch, and here you are embracing me. Glad to have been agreeable to you, at the risk of breaking your limbs. I don't know two of your sort. As for the punch, I wouldn't have returned it, word of honor; you don't have the strength to fight a Hercules like me."

I looked at him attentively while he was speaking. I had tears in my eyes and could hardly contain my agitation. "You don't recognize me!" I said to him, in an emotional voice.

"In truth, no."

"Well, I recognize you, and in twenty days I'll recognize you again, for you've saved my life. It was your kind words that prevented me from committing a cowardly act; they were what rendered me the energy and courage to live; and it's your purse, which I still have on my person," I continued, showing it to him, "that permitted me to satisfy my immediate needs, and gave me the hope of vanquishing my ill-fortune."

"Wait a minute," he said, examining my more closely in his turn, "I've got it, I've got it! It's you who rescued that big dog the other night. It's true that I prevented you from taking a bath in the Seine in perpetuity. That's quite simple, that! A handsome young fellow like you, it would have been a pity to see you lying on Père Thirion's marble bed In the Morgue. But you already have this," he said, touching his heart. "You threw your arms around me when you recognized me, in spite of the carp-jump I just made you take on the sidewalk. You can see, then, that I had the right idea. And now," he added, extending his huge hand, put it there—you have one friend more."

He was about to quit me; I held him back. "No, no," I said to him. "Our acquaintance can't remain there. Firstly, I want you to know to whom you rendered a service; secondly, I'm in your debt and I intend to acquit myself."

"Nonsense, nonsense," the worthy man replied. "You can't have made a fortune in a few days; we'll settle up when you're rich!"

"But I am…an unexpected inheritance…and one of my first cares would have been to come and find you at the address you gave me.

"Well," he said, "I've got an idea. If you're not proud, come and have soup with us at Mère Bonnefoi's place. Oh, you'll be received with a good heart, and we can chat at our ease."

"I accept," I said. "But your time is precious…and what about your work!"

"My work? Oh, I can do without that. I'm thinking of retiring from the estate. At present, I do my carrying as an amateur, and if I still carry my two hundred kilos, it's to maintain my spine, and that's all."

We set forth, and while walking, I told him a part of my story. I saw him wipe away a tear from time to time when I talked about the miseries of my childhood and the privations I'd endured.

We arrived in the port, where the worthy fellow lived.

"Hey, Mame Bonnefoi," he shouted, as he went into a ground-floor room. "Here's a new friend I'm bringing you…"

A stout maternal woman, pink-faced and good-humored, immediately appeared and gave me a superb curtsy.

"Oh, no ceremony," said the mariner. "But for me, this fellow would no longer be in the world; you can see that he belongs to me a tad. Set a place for him; he's an honest lad, whom I've begun to love as if he were family." Addressing me, he said; "I'll tell you the menu: cabbage soup and fish cooked in wine, as only Mère Bonnefoi known how. She has a reputation throughout Bercy, and it'll make you lick your chops."

We sat down at table.

For me, it was a calm in the midst of all the tempest that had assailed me in the last few days.

"I haven't always been on the port," Bonnefoi told me, "after having emptied his third bottle of Beaugency. I had a profession less hard than that one in my youth. I carried love letters scented with musk and many other nice odors to pretty ladies, instead of carrying sacks of wheat and coal or rolling wine-barrels. I was a commissionaire in a fine quarter of Paris, where there was no shortage of the jealous and the amorous.

"One above all never left me short of work, for he was both amorous and jealous. He was paying court to a worthy young woman, sage and pretty enough to eat…the widow of a poor advocate. The dear creature! I can still see her, so happy, when for six months I took her three or four love letters a day. It first it was silver coins that she slipped into my hand, then, later, gold, when she became the mistress of the Chevalier de Saint-Harem…"

"The Chevalier de Saint-Harem!" I cried, interrupting him.

"Yes. A handsome man, believe me, save for his diabolical eyes. I could never look him in the face."

"And the woman! The woman! Tell me her name, I implore you, my friend."

"The woman's name was Henriette Bineau. Poor creature, she had a little boy that she was raising on her own; then, soon she had another child, a girl, by her seducer. But then the letters and the tips became rarer. She never received me without uttering deep sighs. She scarcely dared ask me for news of my customer the Chevalier. 'He isn't coming anymore,' she said to me one day, dissolving in tears. That made me feel bad. I was fond of her; she was so sweet and so good. Two months passed without me being sent to her home. One day I went there on my own account. I learned that she had disappeared, and I've never seen her since."

While listening to the worthy Bonnefoi, enlightenment dawned on me.

Hazard had taken charge of dissipating my doubts and uncertainties. Henriette Bineau really was the daughter of the Chevalier de Saint-Harem!

"The times became bad for the amorous and commissionaires," Bonnefoi continued. "I was joined by two colleagues sporting medals. The disgusted me with the profession, and I came to establish myself in the port, where my back and my arms have earned me a small fortune."

"Your story has interested me more than you'd believe," I told my host. "Now it's necessary for me to leave you. This is my address. Come to see me as soon as possible and as often as possible. Permit me to return your purse," I added, after having adroitly slipped into it, without him perceiving it, a five hundred-franc bill, "and always keep it as a souvenir of my sincere amity and my eternal gratitude."

We embraced cordially, and I went back to my house, very happy with my discovery.

It was nine o'clock when I got back.

Three people were waiting for me: Maître Bridaine, Junon and the doctor. It was a matter of hearing the reading of Monsieur de Saint-Harem's testament, in which the advocate had announced to us that we were personally interested.

That testament, which only death had prevented the Chevalier from destroying, had been picked up by Maître Bridaine from my uncle's bed.

Thus, after having solemnly put on his spectacles, the worthy lawyer acquainted us with the contents of that important document:

I, Hector de Saint-Harem, Chevalier de Malte, in complete liberty of mind and conscience, appoint Maître Bridaine as my testamentary executor, and enjoin him to supervise the strict and entire accomplishment of my last will.

I bequeath to my nephew Albert Dumesnil, the son of my sister, all that I possess in this world: my movable and immovable property, lands, town house, houses, income, silverware, jewels and paintings.

This donation is made on the following conditions.

Firstly, Albert Dumesnil, my heir, will take care of my cat Freyschutz just as I have taken care of him myself during my lifetime. He shall be served every day with healthy and abundant nourishment. He shall be left free in all his actions. If, however, some amorous passion resounds at an undue hour outside the house, my nephew

61

will immediately set out in search of him and bring him
back to the domicile, by force if necessary.

At this point there was a stifled burst of laughter on the part of the doctor, who found the mission with which my uncle was charging me rather strange.

"Monsieur," said Maître Bridaine, severely, "all the wishes of a dead man are respectable, and his heirs must submit to them."

Then he replaced his spectacles, which he had removed in order to admonish the doctor, and continued:

Secondly, if Freyschutz falls ill, I instruct my heir
immediately to summon my own physician, Dr. Hubert.

This time, the doctor was about to protest, but the advocate cut him off by reading the following:

I bequeath to Dr. Hubert, in anticipation of the vis-
its that will be requested of him in the circumstance
foreseen above, my most beautiful ring, ornamented with
a solitaire valued at a thousand écus.

Thirdly, if by negligence, blows, wounds, ill-
treatment or lack of surveillance on the part of my heir,
Freyschutz dies, I want, intend and order that after ex-
amination and proof of the abovementioned facts, that
my nephew Albert Dumesnil be deprived of my inher-
itance, and I then bequeath my entire fortune to the So-
ciety for the Protection of Animals.

Fourthly, I beg Maître Bidaine, my advocate, to ac-
cept as a souvenir of my future gratitude, for the mission
with which I am charging him, the sum of fifteen thou-
sand francs, which I have put on deposit in his safe, and
which he shall consider henceforth as belonging to him.

Lastly, I bequeath to my cook Junon, firstly, every-
thing that she has stolen from me during my lifetime, and
an additional income of six hundred francs per year.

Made this, etc...

Signed: Hector de Saint-Harem.

VIII. The Beggar

Far from getting carried away with regard to the first part of the legacy made to her, Junon contented herself with smiling and saying:

"Necessary to pardon the poor man—he was so weak in the head."

I was consternated by what I had just heard. I was doubtless rich, but on what a condition! The perpetual surveillance of a malevolent animal that must hold me in horror; the affiliation of sorts with it; the responsibility for its life that weighed upon me: all of that seemed horrible, odious and impossible.

I was on the point of renouncing everything, and refusing the insensate life that the testament created for me, and preferring my present poverty, but an idea came to mind, or rather to heart: an idea so tender and generous at the same time that I immediately made my resolution.

And I replied to Maître Bridaine, who was congratulating me on my new fortune: "I shall strive to be worthy of my uncle's generosity by conforming to all the duties that he imposes upon me."

"I defy you to do that," said Junon, with the liberty of language that old domestics arrogate. "It's three days since the animal disappeared from the house."

"A search will be mounted," said Maître Bridaine, "and if, in spite of our efforts, he can't be found, Monsieur Dumesnil will then be discharged of the obligations to which he is submitted by the testament, and his uncle's heritage will be no less acquired."

"In the contrary case," added Dr. Hubert, ironically, as he took his leave, "You'll be the governor of the cat and I'll be its physician; but beware of the scratches of your ward and my client."

"Keep that testament preciously," said Maître Bridaine to me as he left. "Your uncle left other heirs, who are disposed, I know, to contest its value."

"And what do you think of those pretentions?" I asked the advocate.

"I think that we'll triumph over them easily, testament in hand. We'll prove that an old man can have a mania without being insane for that; in any case, all those who knew Monsieur de Saint-Harem will certify his common sense and his reason—but don't lose the will. If that document were to go astray, your adversaries would depreciate it and falsify its terms before the law, and you might be stripped of your inheritance."

I was installed that same evening by the old advocate in the Chevalier de Saint-Harem's town house; but I intended to sleep for one more night in my mansard—to the great despair of Junon, who claimed that a master possessing an annual income of thirty thousand francs ought not to be lodged in a grain-loft.

A quarter of an hour had gone by since Maître Bridaine's departure.

With my eyes half-closed, sitting in the Chevalier's old Voltaire armchair, I was dreaming about Mademoiselle Henriette. I no longer doubted here origin; I rejoiced in advance in the ease and wellbeing that I was going to offer her.

I saw in the milieu of that sleepless dream, the young florist in healthy lodgings, well-lighted, well-ventilated, looking after her delicate health, gradually recovering the color that suffering and labor had stolen from her.

Ought I to say, also, that I saw myself next to her, holding one of her white hands in mine, listening to her soft voice thanking me for having repaired the forgetfulness of the man who had so cruelly abandoned her and her poor mother?

I was allowing myself to be gently lulled by all those cheerful hopes when my attention was attracted toward a sort of niche accommodated in the woodwork of the bookshelves.

It was there that the Chevalier de Saint-Harem, a distinguished bibliophile, buried the pamphlets and valueless books that he judged unworthy of figuring in his precious collection.

There was a slow and repetitive movement inside that redoubt.

The tapestry that closed it agitated insensibly at first, and then with little curt and abrupt shocks, as if the being that the cavity enclosed did not have the strength to push back the light curtain.

I approached it, hesitantly.

Was it a presentiment?

I experienced the same dread that had gripped me every time I approached the Chevalier.

Tremulously, I lifted the curtain, which was then immobile, and I perceived Freyschutz lying on a pile of books and papers, limbs outstretched, head tilted, and swollen tongue dangling. His intense and flamboyant gaze was dull and veiled.

Junon appeared in the doorway of the library.

"He's found!" I cried to her.

"Who?" said the woman. "The cat?"

"Yes, yes, the cat," I replied, with a poignant emotion. "The cat...or another!"

Freyschutz would simply have run the danger of dying of thirst and hunger if he had remained a few hours longer in the depths of his hiding-place.

Had hazard taken him there? Had he been shut in the library by the closure of the doors of the house strictly prescribed by Maître Bridaine after the removal of the deceased?

Or perhaps...but fear took hold of me at that idea; Had the Chevalier's soul, ashamed of its new dwelling, wanted to change it at any price, by letting the wretched creature that it animated perish of starvation?

Come on, come on, I said to myself, making an effort to collect myself, *that's veritable madness. My uncle dreamed up all the chimeras with which he cradled my childhood; his soul is now inhabiting another world, not the body of that feline.*

As for him, nothing is simpler than what has happened; he was thought to be dead when he was only stunned; when the faint passed, he resumed movement and life.

I delivered myself to those reflections while Junon, on my orders, brought the dying animal a saucer of milk, which he drank avidly.

"What did you want from me," I asked the woman, "when you first came into the room?"

"I wanted to tell Monsieur that I've prepared the late master's room for him, and that he can sleep there tonight."

"Never! I'll never live in it!" I cried. "That room will remain closed; no one will lodge in it."

I had scarcely uttered those words than an exclamation from the old maidservant caused me to turn swiftly in her direction, and I saw her pale and trembling before Freyschutz, who had just quit his retreat and was nestling in a soft armchair.

"Oh, my God!" she murmured. "What do I see? Is it really possible? Those eyes…the cat's eyes…one might think that they were Monsieur le Chevalier's!"

Those words rendered me all my terrors; even the servant had been struck by the resemblance.

"I'll never be able to look it in the face," she continued. "It will always seem to me that it's our master who is looking at me."

"Well," I said to her, seeking to reassure her with my voice, which was trembling involuntarily, "let that idea inspire better sentiments for it than those you have had until now. You heard what my uncle demands of me. Have generosity and pity for the animal. After all," I added, carried away by the disorder of my mind, and talking to myself, "what if Monsieur de Saint-Harem's doctrines were true? What if the purest part of us, the ethereal essence that quits us after our death, were forced to go give life to other matter? What if that prodigy, finally, has just been realized in this instance? By how many cares and attentions should I not seek to expiate the cruel action I committed?"

A shrill mewl from Freyschutz seemed to respond to my words, as if he were rejecting angrily the generous sentiments that I had expressed…

Junon was not listening to me, absorbed in her contemplation of Freyschutz. Suddenly, she said: "If we were at one of those theaters where animals become men and men, in their turn…I'd believe that our master has become that cat!"

And with those words the cat launched at the black woman a gaze so fulminating that the poor servant, losing her head, fell to her knees before him and cried: "Bounty of Heaven! If you're my master, order me, command me; I'll always be your faithful servant. First, shall I serve your mash?"

I felt my head weakening in the presence of all these strange scenes. Blood rose to my face; my hands were cold; my pulse was beating a hundred times a minute.

I went out of the house. I walked for a long time under the galleries of the Place Royale, and night fell without my having perceived it.

I was traversing the least illuminated part of the arcades when an individual hidden behind one of the massive pillars approached me and said: "Help me, bourgeois. I'm hungry."

That voice struck me with surprise. I recognized it without being able to recall where I had heard it. I took a few paces, followed by the beggar, but, having arrived in the luminous zone projected by a street-lamp, I cast my eyes on the unknown man and found myself confronted by Mademoiselle Henriette's brother.

"What! It's you!" he exclaimed, in the impudent tone that had already shocked me. "Too bad, I'd have done better to address myself to someone else, but in the new estate I'm in today, one can't always choose one's customers."

"And you're reduced to asking for alms?" I said.

"Well, when appetite knocks on the door without one being able to open it…it's been twenty-four hours since I've had a bite to eat."

"But what about your sister, wretch?"

"You heard," he replied. "She told me straight that she'd refuse to feed me in future."

"What about the money she gave you?"

"Two portraits of the monarch at a hundred sous apiece, that's a fine affair. It's the Ablette who devoured them."

"Who's the Ablette?"[7]

"My mistress," he continued, swelling up with pride. "The lady dear to my heart; a lovely girl who has a good profession. She poses for shoulders in painters' studios, but it appears that shoulders aren't paying much at the moment. Artists are asking for torsos, and the Ablette can't eat that bread. Shoulders as much as you like, but *zut* for the rest."

He appeared to weaken as he pronounced the last words, and leaned against the pillar next to which we were talking."

Pity came to my soul. That depraved creature was no less than Henriette's brother, and I felt that I couldn't abandon him in that frightful misery."

"Come on, come with me," I said to him.

"Where to?"

"My house, a few steps away. I'll give you the nourishment of which you appear to have a pressing need."

"Truth to tell, my pins will no longer carry me."

"Well then, take my arm and lean on me."

"That's quite an honor you're doing me, Monsieur," he said, changing his tone and touching his cap.

"Walk, walk, and let's not waste time." I supported him as far as my door and took him into the house.

---

[7] An *ablette* is a small freshwater fish, usually known in English as a bleak. It was once of some commercial interest because its scales were used in the manufacture of artificial pearls.

At the sight of my strange companion, Junon was bewildered. "Who's that you're bringing?" she said.

"What does it matter to you?" I replied, ill-humoredly. "Serve Monsieur what you've prepared for me."

"Well! And what about you?"

"I won't have anything this evening. I'm suffering, and only need rest."

Junon set the table and I made the young beggar sit down. He drank and ate moderately, and when he had recovered his strength somewhat, I said to him: "Let's see, do you want to go now, or chat with me for a few minutes?"

"I'd rather chat," he replied, eyeing a respectable bottle of wine that the woman had placed on the table.

I poured him a glass of old Bordeaux. He drank it with a comical bliss, saying: "Père Lathuile hasn't the like," and then clicking his tongue. "Now, he continued, leaning on the table, "chat away. I'm listening."

IX. Race Across the Rooftops

"Would you like to change your life," I asked my guest without preamble, "accept a laborious occupation and acquire a serious status?"

"Well, if you're proposing that of peer of France, I can only gain by the swap."

"It's not a joking matter," I said, in a benevolent but severe tone. "Your sister inspires a keen interest in me. Not the one you supposed when you encountered me in her home; but a discovery I've made, and which I'll tell you later, gives me the right—a sacred right, you understand—to change her situation, to create a gentle and happy life for her, and you're too closely related to her for a part of the interest I have not to rebound on you."

"Don't understand," was his only response.

"You'll understand in due course; let it suffice for now for you to know that I'd like to see you emerge from the unfortunate path you've taken. I could have contented myself, when you extended your hand to me just now, to drop a few coins into it, but that money would have gone to find that which your sister has so often given you. I want to do more for you than that."

"It's true," he interrupted, "that if you want to re-load the ship, you have to move the packages furiously. First of all, I don't have any clothes to put on my back, and I can't present myself at Court in this costume. My smock resembles a skimmer, and my trousers are nearly becoming indecent."

"You'll have clothes and everything you lack; you'll be suitably dressed, well-lodged, well-nourished, and you'll have a wage of two hundred francs a month, of which I'll give you the first quarter tomorrow."

"A millionaire! I'm a millionaire!" he exclaimed, rising to his feet and attempting a grotesque dance-step in my dining room. Then, that moment of mad joy having passed, he returned tranquilly to sit facing me, and said: "Come on, no joking. It's not good to make fun of poor folk like that."

"I'm not making fun of you," I replied, "and I intend to do everything I promise you, but there are certain conditions to my benefits."

"There's the snag," said the gamin. "What are they?"

"To abandon your bad acquaintances and change your conduct. I hope you've only gone astray and aren't vicious. I'll place you in an honest establishment, and you'll only have good examples before your eyes. First of all, you'll learn to speak another language than the ignoble argot with which you're familiar. If your nature is good, as I'd like to suppose, you'll soon blush at your past, you'll regret it. Then I'll occupy myself with your future, and it won't depend on me whether it's solid and happy."

As I spoke, I saw a singular change take place in my interlocutor. His savage physiognomy softened, his features were painted with a new emotion; his gaze had an expression of sadness and shame at the same time.

He turned his head to hide it from me, and I saw the sleeve of his smock pass rapidly over his eyes.

"Look," he said to me, suddenly, "I'm a rogue, a frightful rogue, that's the way it is, but all the same, what you've just said, that stirs my heart. Since the old abbé who gave me my first communion six years ago, nobody's talked to me like that; my sister gives me a sermon from time to time, but it seems so funny in her mouth that I laugh in her face, while you, you make me want to weep. Oh, don't think I'm saying all this because of what you might do for me, you could do nothing and it would be the same. And if you want...but I'd never dare ask you that..." And he stopped.

"Speak, speak," I said to him.

"Well, if you want to make me happy and prove to me that you don't despise me too much, you could give me your hand."

I extended mine, and he shook it vigorously.

"Now," he said, energetically, "that's the bargain sealed. Make of me what you please; I belong to you, body and soul; I'll obey you like your valet, like your dog..." At the last word his face darkened. "Oh yes," he added, "about the dog...I behaved like a real scoundrel with ours, but thanks to you, poor Fidele was saved, and my little sister will forgive me."

There was such a tone of repentance in his words that I was touched.

"I'll take charge of that," I told him, "and I'll make your peace with Mademoiselle Henriette."

"Ah!" he said. "It's good to chat, but it's necessary to sleep, and I risk being pinched by the cops if I go back to my usual domicile this evening."

"And what is that domicile?"

"A coal-barge in the port, damn it. The bed's hard but the accommodation's gratis."

"You'll sleep here," I told him.

"Here, in a real bed?"

"In a real bed."

"With a mattress?"

"A complete bed, in a room in this house."

"Not possible. Good God, not possible! Me, who's been sleeping rough for two months!"

"Come on, come on," I continued. "This house, which was bought fully furnished, contains several rooms that have never been occupied; you can spend the night in one of them."

My new guest followed me up to the third floor, where I resided, but as I went past my room to go to the one I destined for him I was astonished to see my door open.

I went in, candle in hand, and I perceived Freyschutz crouching next to the table on which I normally wrote, holding in his claws an object that he was trying to tear to pieces.

That object was a parchment envelope sealed in black, from which a piece of paper was beginning to escape that seemed to be the objective of the animal's aggression. I immediately recognized my uncle's testament, which, by virtue of an unfortunate distraction, I had forgotten on that table,

I ran toward the feline in order to snatch it away from him, but, quicker and more agile than me, he launched himself toward the door, went through it and briskly climbed the stairs that led to the attic of the house, holding the important document between his teeth.

"I'm doomed!" I cried, beside myself. "That piece of paper is my entire fortune!"

"And it's that beast that's carrying it off?" said the gamin, who had seen everything. "Well, it's necessary to get it back, at all costs." And a single bound took him on to the stairway, in pursuit of the cat.

I followed him, but my emotion was so strong that I could hardly climb the steps, and it seemed to me during that time that a mysterious voice murmured in my ear my uncle's sinister dying words:

"I don't know what new existence is reserved for me, but be certain that my hatred will pursue you constantly and relentlessly."

At the moment when I arrived in the attic, preceded by Henriette's brother, the latter showed me a skylight opening on to the roofs and said to me, with a consternated expression: "It went that way."

"Impossible to pursue him by that path," I cried, despairingly.

"For you, perhaps—you're too big and too strong," he said, delightedly, "but rats can slide anywhere, and I'm a rat, me, I can get through the ventilation-shaft of a cellar. That window's like a coaching-door to me. Let's go," he added, hanging from the side of the skylight. "For a good cat, a good rat."

Then, hoisting himself up to the window-sill with a gymnastic flip, he introduced his legs into the narrow opening; his upper body followed the legs outside, and he was on the sloping roof, where he could only maintain himself by clinging to the worm-eaten frame of the skylight.

"Damn," he said. "It's a matter of turning round now and walking on four feet, like the damned thief I'm chasing."

That act of courage had been accomplished so rapidly that I had not had time to oppose it.

"Come back! Come back!" I shouted, fearfully. "No fortune is worth a man's life, and I'd rather be ruined a thousand times over than expose you to such dangers."

"It's your own fault," he said, "for being so good to me."

And so saying, he turned round slowly and set himself belly down on the roof.

I uttered a cry of alarm.

"Have no fear," he said. "I've done the trapeze."

But at that moment, the frame of the skylight, on to which he was holding, rotted by time and damp, broke in his hand, and I saw him slide rapidly down the sloping roof and disappear from my sight.

Gripped with horror, I leaned half my body out of the skylight, and perceived him lying against a vast brick chimney-stack, whose massive and heavy construction had stopped him in his fall.

Stunned for a few seconds, he was soon on his feet again, and I was able to hear the words: "Vile beast, I'll catch you or I'll leave me bones here!"

Then I watched the most terrible scene one could ever see.

A bright moon illuminated an entire horizon of tiles and slates, and on that new and perilous racecourse a man, little more than a child, deployed an audacity, an art and an agility that the cleverest of acrobats would have envied, sometimes walking along the crest of a roof, then letting himself slide from an elevated house to a lower one, taking advantage of the slightest cracks and projections that he encountered on his route, supporting himself on anything that came to hand: a jutting brick, or the end of a beam emerging from a wall.

And in the meantime, the cat was running, climbing, leaping, seemingly mocking the bold hunter, sometimes stopping in inaccessible places as if to challenge him to pursue him there; launching himself into a maze of pipes of every sort, weather-vanes and chimney-stacks of various forms, crowded like the masts of ships in port.

He sometimes disappeared, to reappear thereafter on one to those elevated promontories, where his enemy could not rejoin him.

But soon, an incident of that disordered chase rendered it even more frightening.

X. The Gargoyle

In his strategic course, Freyschutz bumped into an obstacle, and nearly lost his equilibrium; and in that sudden commotion, the envelope that he was holding clenched between his jaws escaped, turned over for a few seconds in the air, and fell on to the sill of a casement situated ten meters below him.

Henriette's brother uttered an exclamation of joy. It was no longer a matter of anything but reaching the precious piece of paper and taking possession of it.

But how? By what route, by what means could he reach it?

The simplest way, assuredly, would have been to come back to the attic of the, climb back in, run down swiftly to the street, go and knock on the house next door and reclaim what the wind had pushed on to one of its windows.

That project had scarcely been formed, and I was about to realize it, when, with an immense fright, I saw what I am about to recount.

Either because the aerial voyager feared that the cat, more agile than him, might succeed in recovering his prey before he was able to reach it, or because my plan had not occurred to him, he conceived another, which he immediately put into execution.

At that moment he was in a rather large gutter, the extremity of which terminated in a sculpted stone gargoyle, such as one can still see in the ancient monuments of Paris, and which projected from the exterior of the roof for the flow of rainwater. He had the idea of utilizing that projection to reach the casement on the floor below, which was ornamented by a narrow balcony.

The windows of that house, which was under repair, had no shutters as yet; nothing would be easier, therefore, once on that balcony, than to go by way of the interior of the house to the place where the object of his pursuit lay.

The perils of that reckless trajectory did not stop him.

Having suspended himself by his hands from the gargoyle, which surpassed the roof by some three feet, he allowed his body to float for a few seconds in mid-air, while his feet sought to encounter the window on which he wanted to place himself.

I trembled that he might not find it, or that his fatigued arms would lose their grip, but something far more horrible than what I feared occurred.

The ornament of Medieval sculpture by means of which the unfortunate young man was supporting himself suddenly began to tilt and buckle, twisting under the weight that it was supporting. The ancient stone gargoyle had been replaced by a gargoyle made of lead; the metal gradually extended, stretching from second to second.

I divined that at the moment when, by virtue of the force of tension, the support would have assumed a vertical position, the rupture would become inevitable, and the unfortunate fellow would be precipitated into the void.

My anticipations were realized.

A crack was heard, and that lead salmon of sorts parted violently from its mount.

But Providence was watching over the courageous child!

At the moment when the heavy mass was about to drag him down and crush him in its fall, he felt something floating against his face. It was a thick and solid rope, the knotted cord of a plasterer's apparatus. He released the support, grabbed the rope with a desperate clutch, clung on to it with all the energy that the hope of salvation in the presence of death gives, and, defying destiny, he slid down it rapidly until he encountered a solid surface, on which he stopped.

From the moment when the gargoyle broke, I could no longer see anything. A bloody cloud passed over my eyes, and I was only extracted from my daze by the resounding noise that the leaden device made as it crashed into the pavement.

Distraught, almost mad, I hurtled out of the attic, went down to the street and ran to the house next door, where that terrible scene had unfolded. I expected only to find a cadaver, and I searched for the place where Henriette's brother had been precipitated.

A burst of joyful laughter resounded above my head.

"Don't look there, on the ground!" the gamin shouted to me. "I'm here, I'm lodging on the first floor like a banker in the Chaussée-d'Antin."

I raised my eyes, and I perceived him astride the window-sill on to which the wind had carried my uncle's testament.

I uttered a cry of joy.

"Well, it pleases you that I'm not splattered," he shouted. "At least that proves that you already love me a little. But the paper, the accursed paper—you're not asking me about that?"

"I was only thinking of you," I said, "of you, who risked your life for me, and I don't care about my ruination, since you're safe."

"Thanks, thanks," he said, in an emotional voice. "Any more words like that and my eyes will change into the fountain of the Innocents, but I don't want you to languish. Here," he said, waving the envelope with a triumphant expression, "here's the blessed scribble that the devil filched. That's what comes of having been at Franconi's; I do gymnastics like Monsieur Auriol. Roll up, roll up, Messieurs, Mesdames, come and see the incomparable Mimi Taloche,[8] descending from the third floor with a plasterer's rope. It's true that I haven't taken a bow, but one can't think of everything at these moments."

"Come down, come down," I said to him. "I need to embrace you."

"If it's a matter of that, I'll quit my mount and be there in a tick."

I went to meet him and he fell into my arms. I perceived then that he had just fainted.

The strange fluency of the Parisian gamin had sustained him until then, the eccentric bluster—if I might be permitted the expression—that inoculates those poor creatures in infancy, had combated momentarily the terrible emotions through which he had just passed. But nature, put to excessive proof, regained the upper hand, and the young man, so firm and so intrepid in danger, weakened as soon as the peril no longer existed.

---

[8] *Taloche* has several meanings in Parisian argot, the most common one referring to a cuff, both in the sense of the end of a sleeve and a blow, but it can also mean the implement with which a plasterer smoothes his work.

The Parisian gamin is a type that is encountered nowhere else than in Paris; it is a special product of that city, where fortune, poverty, genius, ignorance, virtue and depravity mingle and are confounded more than in any other city in Europe.

Here, the children of the people are almost always born intelligent. Gallic verve is their godmother; but the bitterness of their childhood, family poverty, unsatisfied needs, the sight of the luxury of the rich, their prodigality, their joys and their celebrations, develop in those creatures a continuous sentiment of envy, which is re-lived by irony and sarcasm.

Their language is picturesque, vivacious and color-ful; they do not seek phrases to depict a defect, a vice or a folly; they photograph it in a word, and that word is often so accurate that it becomes popular in spite of its vulgarity. The gamins of Paris have augmented French vocabulary more than all the members of the Académie.

Oh, how many serious things there are to say about those wretched adolescents! How many honest things there are to do to purify that young mire of our popula-tion!

When our heroic gamin opened his eyes again he was lying in a good bed: one of those beds that he had desired so much, had dreamed about so frequently.

"How are you feeling?" I asked him.

"My limbs are creaking like a wooden puppet's," he replied, "And as for my head, it's so heavy that one might think that that old vagabond of a lead gargoyle had dived into it. What about your paper," he continued, urgently. "Did you get it back while my eyes were shut?"

"Here it is; and this time, it will no longer quit my person."

"That's all right, then," he said, with a malicious smile. "Once I'm on my feet, I'll pay my debt."

"To whom?"

"To the cat, of course. That animal's more evil than my former client, the royal tiger at the Jardin des Plantes. It looked at me from time to time with eyes so frightful that two or three times, I nearly lost my equilibrium. So I'll take care of it; it'll have a first class funeral in the rag-picker's hut."

"Wretch! You're going to kill it?"

"And without putting gloves on to do it. Two good pinches of arsenic in its soup, and the Rominagrabis will have joined its ancestors."[9]

"You won't do anything of the sort!" I said, full of terror.

"Why not?" he said, becoming animated. "A nasty beast that nearly made me break my neck—I'll say that it was rabid. Twenty sous reward—that's the price, but I'll grant the government mercy and I'll get rid of him for you gratis."

"I forbid it! I'll never see you again as long as you live, if you do such a thing."

"That's a bit strong! Why, then?"

"Because," I cried, involuntarily, as if seized by vertigo, "because in killing that cat you'd be murdering..." But I fled without pronouncing the word that was hovering on my lips.

The action that my uncle's favorite had just committed had a character so perfidious, so considered, so wickedly human, that it appeared to me to be impossible

---

[9] The gamin is presumably thinking of Raminagrobis, the name of a poet in Rabelais, appropriated by Jean de La Fontaine for the name of a cat in one of his fables.

to attribute it merely to the malevolent nature of the animal.

Lacépède, Buffon, Cuvier and Daubenton accord an interior sense to animals. That sense gives them the perception of things that are useful or contrary to them. It is for that reason that we see certain quadrupeds—dogs, for example—finding in a meadow the sprig of herb that will soothe their suffering or reestablish the equilibrium of their health.

As for the good or bad qualities of animals, their character varies with their species; the dog is good and devoted, the cat ingrate, a traitor and a thief. One caresses a child of which it is often the martyr; the other scratches pitilessly at the slightest dolor it is made to feel.

But, even given that a cat is ingeniously evil, could I admit that simple instinct could enable one to discover, among twenty papers placed on my table, the one whose destruction would cause a prejudice to its possessor?

That is what troubled my reason, what forced me to recognize, under that bestial envelope, a cruel and hostile intelligence, persisting in its projects of hated and vengeance, of which only the soul of the Chevalier could be culpable toward me.

While making those strange reflections, I headed for the abode of the young florist. There alone I hoped to find a little calm and relief. It seemed to me that at the pleasant sight of her, my terrors would vanish and my thoughts would be disengaged from the limbo in which they were retained.

Then again, I wanted to talk to her about her father, the father whose faults and neglect I had the holy mission of repairing.

I was in a hurry to extract the poor child from her miserable life, to create a happy future for her, which she merited so thoroughly; and it was in that state of mind that I arrived at Henriette's home.

XI. Evidence

"It's you?" said Henriette, when she opened the door of her redoubt to me—and a vivid blush colored her pale cheeks, like the setting sun when it pierces the clouds that are hiding it.

"It's me. I'd like to talk for you for a few moments."

"Only a few moments?" she said. "That's very little, especially after the ascent you've just made—one needs rest."

"It's just that I'm afraid of taking up your time and preventing you from working."

"Oh, I have time. Here, sit down facing me, on the other side of my little table. Just be careful of what I have on top of it: my colors, my brass wire, my batiste flowers, already cut out. Oh, mine is very meticulous work."

"And it isn't well-paid?" I said.

"But yes…quite well…I have the room, and I earn nearly forty francs a month."

"And you live on that meager sum?"

"Well, very nearly. I need so little, especially now that I'm alone."

She retained a sigh in pronouncing those words. I divined that the sigh was in regard to the wicked brother whom she had been obliged to send away, whom that child had virtually raised, and whom she could not help loving.

"And then," I said, "it's necessary that you get some air, that you sometimes go out."

"Oh, as little as I can—but I'm obliged to walk Fidele. Look at him, lying at your feet; he seems sad that you're not saying anything to him."

In fact, the poor beast had his large muzzle turned in my direction, and his intelligent eyes seemed to be reproaching me for my indifference.

At the slightest gesture I made, however, he launched himself toward me, placing his two enormous forepaws on my knees, and in his joyful enthusiasm he nearly knocked over the florist's little table.

"Now, now, Monsieur Fidele!" said Henriette. "You nearly spoiled a masterpiece! You don't know, then, that all these beautiful roses, these jasmines and these daisies are to give you bones to chew, to make the good soup that you love so much?"

Fidele, ashamed of being scolded by his mistress, went to lick her pink fingertips, and then came back to stand by me.

"Has it been a long time," I asked, "since you've seen your brother?"

"You know very well," she replied, emotionally, "that I've forbidden him to come back here. Look, I'll be frank; I've wept a good deal since that sad day, and my eyes, already so fatigued, had no need of that, for an old physician in the house told me that if I continue to work by night I might go blind."

"Oh, my God!" I cried. "But in that case, it's necessary to stop, and stop immediately!"

"It's necessary to live, Monsieur," she replied. "Oh, if my brother, who is two years older than me, had followed my advice, if he'd become sage and laborious, we would have stayed together, and with his work and mine, we could have been happy and supported us both."

"Well," I told her, "I've seen your brother again, and between the two of us, perhaps we'll render him worthy of you one day."

Then I told her everything that had happened.

During my narration, the charming girl was hardly breathing; soon, her features were full of alarm, and then her pretty face was covered in tears, agitated and palpitating, until she had hard the end of my story.

Immediately, putting her hands together, she said, with the most tender fervor: "Oh my God! How good you are to have conserved him for me!"

"He has courage," I said, "and a generous heart, if I can judge it by the few sentiments he's allowed me to see. I've contracted a debt of gratitude to him and I shall acquit it, I hope, by making him a laborious man and an honest one."

"Oh, Monsieur," she continued, expressively, "since the first moment you entered my room, you've brought me nothing but joy. But at least tell me to whom I owe these benefits?"

"Mademoiselle," I replied, smiling, "Have you ever read fairy tales?"

"Yes, yes, Monsieur, in my childhood; and I dreamed every night about those honest godmothers that protected unfortunate princesses, and the good genies granting all the wishes of those who invoked them."

"Well, what if I were one of those genies, if I had the power to satisfy all your wishes and render you as happy as you deserve to be? What if I could, with a word, give you, to begin with, what your delicate health requires: a bright and salubrious apartment, a mild ease, almost a fortune, which would permit you to renounce your difficult labor and to enjoy, in future, the distractions of your age: to walk in the shade of tall trees, to live in the midst of the beautiful flowers that you imitate so well?

"And what if the good genie who could operate all these prodigies said to you: 'Mademoiselle, I am only rendering to you what belongs to you, and your mother would bless you in Heaven for having accepted all that I am offering you'?"

"My mother?" she said, manifesting the most ardent surprise.

"Your mother, Henriette Bineau, whose name hazard has revealed to me. And as there is always a talisman in fairy tales," I added, "you possess yours in the locket that you showed me."

"But the portrait that it contains…?"

"Is that of your father, you told me—and your father was the Chevalier de Saint-Harem, my uncle."

"What am I hearing?" she cried. "My father! He still exists? Oh, take me to him! Perhaps he won't refuse to see me!"

"He's no longer alive, my poor child," I told her. "We lost him only a few days ago."

Collecting herself for a few moments, she said a brief prayer for the repose of the soul of the man who had abandoned her mother!

"I'm the Chevalier de Saint-Harem's heir," I told her, "his sole heir; and my first duty will be to repair your father's indifference by sharing with you all that I possess."

"No, no," she said, "that's not what he intended. I only wanted two things in this world: to know him and to be loved by him. But since God has not permitted it, I don't want, after his death, a wellbeing that he refused us during his life."

"Mademoiselle," I replied, "after the life of the earth, there is another life; and who knows whether your father might not regret his indifference and his neglect now? Who knows," I added—and I felt myself going pale as I pronounced the words—"whether his soul is not awaiting a repose or relief from the reparation that you are refusing to accept?"

"Oh, if I could believe that," said the gentle creature, "if I were able to give him happiness in Heaven, in spite of all the harm he has done us on earth, I wouldn't hesitate for a moment."

"Well, don't hesitate!" I cried. "Death has its mysteries, which it is not permitted to us to penetrate. Who can tell whether cruel tortures and painful peregrinations might not be spared the soul of the man who gave you the light of day in that fashion? And whether, quitting a shameful prison, it might not launch forth into the ether, where divine forgiveness awaits it?"

A kind of involuntary exaltation had inspired the singular words that I had just pronounced. Henriette, nonplussed, listened to me without comprehension, and I could read a sharp anxiety in her features.

I hastened to reassure her.

"My affection for Monsieur de Saint-Harem sometimes carries me a little far," I said, "but I'm sure that you'll forgive me... So, now, everything is agreed between us, and tomorrow, I'll occupy myself with putting you in possession of your heritage."

"Oh don't do that," she said, putting her little hands together graciously. "I'm so habituated to poverty that such a fortune might make me lose my head. Act as you think appropriate; everything you decide will be for the best; treat me as a sister, for you could never have one more tender and more devoted than me."

"Well," I said, "brothers have family privileges; they can kiss their sisters."

She presented her forehead to me.

That kiss, fraternal as it was, caused her a disturbance that did not escape me.

I felt very emotional myself. I had never been in love, and that first awakening of my heart impressed me vividly.

"Come and see me tomorrow, dear Henriette," I said to her, as I left. "Here is my address. And tomorrow, we'll see about finding you more appropriate lodgings."

"Oh, they'll please me, I'm sure...especially..."

"Especially?"

"Especially if they're not too far away from yours. Listen, then," she continued, smiling. "I'll need a protector, a defender; now that you've made me so rich, I'll be afraid of thieves."

I went away, very pensive and very happy.

"Well," I said to Junon, when I got back to the house, "how is our guest?"

"Who? The dirty fellow who slept here? He's gone out."

"Gone out?"

"But as he went he left this piece of paper for you..."

I took the piece of paper and deciphered, with difficulty, these words, written with an orthography that I shall spare the reader:

I'm going to smarten myself up a bit, thanks to the purse you left me to satisfy my initial needs. I don't want you to blush at me in your house. You'll see me again spick and span.

"What about Freyschutz?" I asked Junon.

"Freyschutz? Oh, he's a funny cat! Now he has Monsieur de Saint-Harem's eyes, one might think he shared all his manias. Monsieur knows how greedy Freyschutz was, and how he filched all the fine morsels he could reach, from this house and he neighbors. Well, I've just found him in our parlor tranquilly lapping his milk alongside a magnificent roasted pullet for Monsieur's dinner. By Saint Junon, my patron, Monsieur le Chevalier would have done the same!"

Junon believed fervently that the wife of Jupiter was a saint in Heaven.

I did not think, as the woman said, that a Knight of Malta would ever have lapped a saucer of milk, but I was struck by the change that had taken place in Freyschutz's tastes, and their analogy with Monsieur de Saint-Harem's repugnance for all animal nourishment.

I was even more surprised by what happened beside me during the maidservant's story.

Since Henriette's brother had returned my uncle's testament to me, recovered with such difficulty, I had taken it out of the envelope that enclosed it and put it in a wallet that never left my possession. But that envelope, still stained by its perilous voyage, was still lying on the floor where I had thrown it.

Being thick, and made of coarse parchment, it still appeared to contain the document that I had prudently extracted from it, and anyone might have been deceived on that score. Freyschutz was doubtless the first dupe, for, after having slyly introduced himself into the library, in the wake of Junon, I perceived him dexterously pushing the envelope that he believed to contain the will, sometimes with the tip of his slender muzzle and sometimes with repeated little thrusts of his paws, all the way to the antique fireplace, where an ardent fire was blazing.

At that sight, I felt a violent anger. That obstinacy in trying to ruin me was a revelation, and dissipated my last doubts. Exasperated, beside myself, losing my head and submitting to the effect of my constant preoccupation, I shouted furiously, without being conscious of what I was saying:

"What you're doing there, Uncle, is infamous!"

The cat launched a profound gaze at me, which penetrated me like a red hot iron to the depths of my heart. Then he disappeared.

As for Junon, she let herself fall into an armchair, saying: "My God, is it possible that that animal is Monsieur le Chevalier?"

XII. A Father is Always a Father

From the moment that I had pronounced the strange words that concluded the previous chapter, Freyschutz fled from me, taking every opportunity to avoid me, and I confess that I was very glad of it.

The sight of him always caused me a sharp emotion, and his calculated distancing provided me with further confirmation of the idea of that astonishing metamorphosis. In any case, admitting that prodigious possibility, our family relationship would have been difficult; our habits were no longer similar, and no uncle and nephew ever found themselves in such an embarrassing situation. Uncles of a difficult, eccentric, miserly and surly character have been seen before, but feline uncles hardly ever.

Sometimes, I perceived the solitary individual hidden under some armchair or perched on the corner of a wall, his head buried in his thick fur. His attitude was so sad, so morose, so dejected, that I felt seized by a keen compassion for him. Then I recalled all my doubts from my memory, and I tried no longer to see in the poor creature anything but the malevolent brute that had always detested me.

As for Junon, she was so imbued with the Chevalier's doctrines, and had heard him repeating so often that human souls change bodies after decease, that she had ended up familiarizing herself with the idea that her master's soul was inhabiting the body of his favorite cat.

"He loved him so much," she added, in support of her opinion.

So, since the words that had escaped me in my anger, there was no care that Junon did not lavish on Freyschutz; it would not have needed much for her to set him a place at the table.

She only approached him respectfully, and never addressed him in other way than Monsieur le Chat.

For his part, he seemed grateful for the attentions of the woman; he was as meek with her as his evil nature permitted, but he did not authorize any familiarity. In trying one day to stroke his back, a caress much appreciated by his peers, the woman was greeted by a mewl so furious that she thought it wise not to try again.

One evening when she served his soup too hot, however, she received a frightful scratch from his claw, and the poor woman ran to me, in tears, to show me her bloody hand, saying: "Look what your uncle has done to me. I've tried to be nice to him, but he's always so surly. Monsieur le Chevalier is definitely not comfortable!"

A few days after my visit, Henriette came in response to my invitation. I was astonished by her lateness in coming to see me, but I divined the cause as soon as she appeared. The poor girl had wanted to spruce herself up a little.

Was it vanity or another sentiment that was guiding her? It did not matter; she was charming in her simple white dress, with her beautiful hair hidden beneath a pretty new straw hat.

I welcomed her not as a stranger but as a relative, and she went crimson on hearing me address her as "Cousin."

The presence of the charming girl in my somber dwelling spread a perfume of youth therein, which was reflected everywhere and in everything. It was spring chasing winter away. The sadness seemed to flee before her; my thoughts became serene again under her soft gaze—or rather, I no longer thought about anything but her; and I said to myself that, since she brought me such calm and wellbeing, I would be very maladroit not to try to fix her close at hand.

I showed her all the vast and numerous rooms of the house.

Only one thing struck her. "Oh my God!" she said. "Not a single flower here? They're jolly good company, though, and flowers don't cost much when one is able to get up early and go to buy them oneself at the morning market."

"Well," I replied. "You shall choose them henceforth." I added, hesitantly: "Would you like to become their gardener one day?"

"Why not?" she said, without understanding the meaning of my proposition. "Oh, I know them, you see, I've lived with them for a long time. Except that you'll permit me to copy them for you sometimes, and that will be more cheerful than all the portraits of these Messieurs, who look so harsh and nasty."

She started laughing in the face of the Chevalier's ancestors; then her face suddenly darkened.

"What's the matter?" I asked.

"I was expecting to find my brother here."

I dared not tell her that he had not reappeared at the house for a week. "He wasn't expecting you, my dear Henriette, and we'll doubtless see him before long."

"He has such a weak character, and so easily led," she said. "But with your advice..."

"And yours," I added. "We'll watch over him, you and I...for you'll live near here. I've found a nice apartment on the boulevard, a short distance away. I've given orders for it to be furnished simply, but with taste. There

97

will even be a cupboard for Fidele, next to your bed-room. It's a rude gendarme that you'll have there to guard you!"

"Oh, how good you are," she said. "You think of everything. But my joy will often be troubled when I think about my poor mother, who died so miserably. Look," she continued, "I've brought you this little album in which my mother wrote her most secret thoughts; you can judge her and know her sad story, written by herself in a few lines."

"Yes, certainly," I said, "but on condition that you read it to me yourself."

She sat down beside me in the library, which I had made into my work room, and commenced thus:

"I was widowed two years ago, still beautiful, I was told, but I rejected all homages, not seeing anyone and only living for my son, my little Auguste, my sole con-solation in this world. I no longer possess anything else. I sold everything to pay my husband's debts. Two months' rent that I was obliged to pay under pain of be-ing evicted from my home took away my last resources.

"One day, I found myself without money, without furniture, without bread, and without an obol to procure me any. 'Mother,' said my son, 'I'm hungry.'

"It's necessary to be a mother to feel what I felt. I went out. I walked at random. I was mad. I could still hear those words in my ears: 'Mother, I'm hungry.' A few loaves of bread were displayed in the window of a baker's shop. There was no one in the shop. Stealing! That was horrible—but the poor child was hungry.

"All my hesitations vanished at that idea…I extend-ed my hand to commit that unworthy action. Another hand took possession of mine. I turned round, full of terror, and I saw a man, still young, with a distinguished manner, who said to me: 'Wretched woman, you were about to steal!'

"'Yes, to steal,' I replied, dazed. 'To steal that my son might live, who might perhaps expire from need.'

"The man went pale on hearing my response. 'Take me to your son,' he said. 'and you'll no longer know a poverty that leads to crime.'

"At the sight of my profound destitution, he gave evidence of a touching pity. He knew who I was, and was good and affectionate toward my son and me. I saw him again often, and then every day.

"That, alas, is where my sins commenced, but I have so cruelly expiated them since that my daughter will forgive me.

"I resisted for a long time, a very long time, but the fear of losing the man I loved madly vanquished my courage and prevailed over my resolution, and for a year, with him, I was the happiest and the most beloved of women.

"One day, I told him that I was going to be a mother. I thought I would see joy burst forth at that news; he received it almost coldly. I expressed my chagrin to him; he excused it by the surprise he had experienced.

"I didn't see him for a week. I had a presentiment that I was threatened by a great misfortune. A worthy commissionaire who appeared to feel sorry for me, for he had divined my suffering, went to the home of the man whose letters he had been bringing me for such a long time. I awaited his return like an accused man awaiting his sentence.

"The commissionaire came back holding a letter. He showed it to me at the end of the street. I was at my window. Oh, the worthy man—I could have kissed him for that kind thought. He ran and handed the precious letter to me. I covered it with kisses. My hand was trembling so strongly that I could scarcely open it.

"This is the letter, my dear Henriette; the stains that you will find there were made by my tears.

"*My dear Henriette*

"*It is a guilty man who is begging you for mercy. I have deceived you. I cannot marry you, as I have promised. I am a Knight of Malta, and my vows prevent me from giving my name to your son.*

"*Our liaison has perhaps lasted too long. It is necessary to put an end to it. Have as much courage as me. I am departing for a long voyage, but I hope to see you when I return*

"*Hector.*

"*P.S. My banker, whose address you know, will give you thirty thousand francs which I have deposited with him for you.*

"The manuscript continues thus:

"I thought I would die on reading those cruel lines, and I only had the courage to live for you, my adored daughter.

"At first I did not want to receive anything from the ingrate who was abandoning me. His benefit horrified me; but poverty came to assail me for a second time, and I went to ask for the funds that had been announced to me.

"The banker had gone bankrupt and everything was lost."

"So," I said to Henriette, "it was in the midst of tears and frightful poverty that you were born. And the Chevalier de Saint-Harem never made enquiries about the child whose father he was?"

"Oh, Monsieur," said Henriette, "don't continue. Let me forget the wrongs that my mother forgave, let me respect the memory of the man to whom I owe life, and for whom I pray to God every day..."

A dolorous mewling was heard.

A tapestry door-curtain that agitated for a few seconds was violently lifted up, and Freyschutz advanced into the middle of the room. Then he stopped, paraded his gaze over Henriette and me, and, approaching the young woman swiftly, he leapt on to her knees.

XIII. The Stretcher

My last doubts vanished on seeing what had just happened.

The Chevalier's soul revealed itself to me in a positive and incontestable fashion.

That soul, once so harsh and so cruel, had been stirred on listening to the reading of the last dolors of Henriette's mother, and in spite of the wretched form that contained it, it experienced nevertheless the remorse of its conduct, and seemed to open itself to the tenderness of paternity.

And yet, on gazing at the group formed by the young woman holding Freyschutz on her knees and caressing him with her pale hand, it appeared to me to be enormous, and almost monstrous, to think that I had before my eyes a family tableau!

"I don't like cats," Henriette said to me, suddenly, "but this one seems to be so good and gentle that it pleased me immediately, and I feel that I could easily become attached to it"

Freyschutz uttered a purr of satisfaction, and licked the pretty hand that was stroking him with his rough tongue.

At that moment, a loud voice was heard in the room preceding the library where we were gathered.

That voice was arguing with Junon, who was refusing admission pitilessly.

"I shall enter, old Mooress," said the visitor. "I haven't come here from the Rapée in this hot weather in order to find a wooden face, and Maître Albert Dumesnil won't forgive you for letting me depart without seeing him."

I had recognized the voice. I opened the door immediately, and the worthy Père Bonnefoi, my savior, ran to me, darting a triumphant glace at Junon.

"Welcome, my worthy friend," I said to him, giving him my hand.

"I knew you'd receive me!" he exclaimed. "It's my jacket that caused the old woman not to want to let me in. Negroes are like dogs; they only like well-dressed people."

Henriette was astonished to see me so familiar with the dock worker.

"Père Bonnefoi," I said to her, "rendered me an enormous service; when you know what I owe him, you'll love him as much as I do. Furthermore, my dear Henriette, hazard sometimes leads to singular encounters: this worthy man is the good—the excellent—commissionaire of whom your mother speaks in the pages you've just read me, and who gave evidence of such a touching pity."

"Oh, Monsieur," said Henriette, whose eyes moistened, "how glad I am to meet you."

"So," said Bonnefoi, "you're the daughter of the poor young woman whom my customer, the wicked Chevalier de Saint-Harem, rendered so unhappy..."

A muffled mewl from Freyschutz seemed to protest against the ill-sounding epithet that the ex-commissionaire had used in regard to the Chevalier.

"...It was necessary to have no heart to act so harshly with that beautiful and gentle creature; but you see, all these rich libertines only know their pleasures. They see an honest and virtuous young woman; they seduce her; they dishonor her; then, the caprice having passed, they leave her flat, neither seen not known, and run in the other direction. Those men are as treacherous as our gutter-cats.

"Oh, forgive me," he exclaimed, cheerfully, on seeing Freyschutz suddenly get up and dart one of his terrible glances at him. "I hadn't noticed Monsieur." And he started laughing, in his frank and joyful fashion."

I remembered the Chevalier's violent and vindictive character, and feared that the cat's claws might do my guest a bad turn, so I proposed to my young friend that we go to visit her new apartment, situated on the boulevard not far from the house."

"Why doesn't she lodge here with you?" said Bonnefoi, "since the poor child has neither parents nor family, and is your cousin, after all—a cousin on the wrong side of the blanket, but none the less so for that. And you see, young women ought not to live alone in our great city of Paris. There are too many Chevaliers de Saint-Harem here."

At that remark, Freyschutz bounded to the floor and launched himself at Père Bonnefoi, who only just had time to fend him off with the stout cane he was holding in his hand.

The cat stopped.

"Ah! What's the matter with that animal?" continued the mariner. "Is it rabid? One might think that it wanted to devour me."

"Come on, Henriette," I said. "My new friend will accompany us, and perhaps I'll ask him to help us with your installation."

"As to that, gladly, and if there's some moving house to do, count on me; Mademoiselle's furniture can't be as heavy as my sacks of wheat or coal."

We were about to cross the threshold of the library when Henriette noticed that Freyschutz was following us.

"Ah," she said to me, "your cat appears to love me as much as my dear Fidele, and I fear that he might become jealous. Stay there!" she added, making a sign of adieu to Freyschutz. "I'll come back, I promise."

And the cat, very sad, went to nestle under an armchair.

It is necessary to have known poverty to comprehend the joy one experiences in emerging from it. On entering into her new abode, Henriette could not have been happier. A palace would not have astonished her and charmed her more.

She ran from room to room, admiring everything, stopping in front of every mirror, in which she looked at herself, rearranging her hair before one and adjusting her dress in front of another.

"But it's too beautiful, too grand or me," she exclaimed. "I could never furnish all these rooms."

"Haven't you appointed me as your business manager, your steward, "I said. "All those concerns are my responsibility. This is your bedroom, overlooking the gardens. Here, adjacent to it, this little cabinet is for Fidele to sleep.

"Then, there's this pretty room that you'll make into your reception room, which we'll decorate with all the lovely flowers that you imitate so well."

"That's all?" she said to me, lowering her yes. "No other room?"

"But you thought just now that there were too many?"

"Yes, no doubt, for me, but for another?"

"What other?" I said, surprised and almost jealous.

"My brother," she continued. "Don't hold it against me—it's stronger than I am. He certainly has his faults, and has given me a great deal of chagrin, but I still love him tenderly. Remember that, although younger than him, I've almost served as his mother, for I had to reason for both of us on my own. I deprived myself for him, he was so delicate in his childhood. Once I nearly lost him to a serious illness. Oh, if that misfortune had happened, I believe that I'd have died of chagrin.

"You thought me very severe, very hard on him, when you met him in my home, but after your departure I reproached myself for a fault…and yet, he was so wicked! But until now, I've had no one in the world to love but him."

"And now?" I said, with a sharp emotion.

"Now," she replied, blushing, "there are two of you."

"Listen to me Henriette; your brother would enjoy a liberty with you, an independence that he might abuse very quickly. He ought to live with me. I thought at first of placing him in some honest house, where he'd have good examples and good advice, but after the service he rendered me, I'd prefer not to be separated from him again."

"Oh," she cried, "How I…"

She did not finish, but my heart had divined what she was about to say. It was the first and greatest joy of my life."

The mariner interrupted those tender expansions. "The day's wearing on," he said, "and the bell for dinner sounded a while ago. Mère Bonnefoi doesn't like to keep the saucepan on the boil for too long, and ours has been on the fire since this morning."

"And if, by chance, you only went home this evening," I said to my new friend, "what would your wife say to that?"

"She'd think that I had urgent work somewhere, and wouldn't get angry about that. Oh, she isn't jealous, Mère Bonnefoi. Anyway," he added, "when one's lugged around a thousand kilos on one's shoulders all day long, one scarcely thinks about deceiving one's wife. And then, a good housekeeper like mine...that would merit the galleys."

"The three of us will dine together," I said, cheerfully, "and we'll take advantage of the end of this beautiful day to give my young cousin a foretaste of the fine walks in the open air and the country that ought to be so good for her health!"

"What," said Bonnefoi, "you, a fine gentleman, wouldn't blush at my workman's clothes?"

I started to laugh. "My friend," I said, "When you met me for the first time under the Arche-Marion, I swear to you that my entire costume wasn't worth as much as one sleeve of that fine jacket you're wearing."

We went out, and we were about to go up the boulevard in order to quit Paris as quickly as possible, when we encountered a group of men and women of the people, surrounding a stretcher covered with canvas, carried by two policemen.

"He's dead," said someone in the crowd, "or not much better."

"What a pity," said a stout housewife. "They say that he's almost a child."

"It's some rich swine who murdered him," shouted a gamin, "because he was paying court to his daughter. They say that he was dressed like a prince."

A strange presentiment seized me, instinctively. I quit Henriette's arm and I approached the litter, of which I tried to lift the enveloping canvas.

"Don't touch!" said one of the policemen. "Prohibited by the police."

"But what if the person you're carrying needs help during the journey?"

"That only concerns us; we have our orders. We obey the commissaire's orders, and that's all"

"And where are you taking the invalid, or the dead man?" I asked.

"Place Royale, Hôtel Saint-Harem."

At those words, Henriette, by virtue of one of the perceptions of the heart that reason cannot explain, launched herself toward the stretcher, snatched away one of the flaps of the sinister envelope, cast her eyes on the person it contained, uttered a scream of fright, and fainted in my arms.

XIV. A Painter's Farce

Singular professions exist in Paris. Among those bizarre and shady estates, that of model is particularly curious to observe.

There are models of both sexes. Modeling is often handed down from father to son and from mother to daughter. Men generally combine that profession with that of wrestler, fairground athlete or acrobat. It is among those various classes that the muscles are most supple, where the body has conquered all its developments since early youth, that artists, whether painters or sculptors, seek their heroes, their gods, their saints and their martyrs, at three francs or a hundred per sitting, according to the physical beauty or the renown of the subjects.

Rarely does a single model pose for the ensemble; one might have the arms of Milo of Crotona and the twisted legs of a basset hound, another a Greek nose, and Olympian beard and the hump on Aesop. A successful Apollo might possess, on his own, the limbs of four or five individuals, not to mention the features of two or three more. It is for the artist to being all those scattered and dissimilar perfections together, and compose a harmonious ensemble.

The venerable old man, the white appendage of whose chin commands respect, is often a frightful drunkard who will go to a nearby tavern to drink the price of two hours of posing for the beard of Socrates. The worthy man never refuses to figure in a play, and, if necessary, to command a cohort. He has been a sapper in the National Guard and talks about his campaigns in the Crimea to the comrades who pay his tab...

The male model, generally rather neglected in his person, takes very particular care of the portion of his physique that is his capital. He speaks of it with pride, and does not refuse to exhibit it to any artist; the rest does not count; that is for the intimacy of the family.

The women, or rather, the young women, for they are the most appreciated in that métier, receive fees much superior to those allowed to the men. And when one thinks of what is required of the resignation of some of them in order to submit to the conditions of the profession, it is astonishing that there are so many of them.

It is also necessary to say, although it might appear improbable, that many of those poor creatures are relatively honest, and only consider their profession as a plastic labor, outside of which the model, becoming a woman again, recovers the delicacy and modesty of her sex. Perhaps those models are not in the majority; at any rate, it is one of them about whom I want to talk to you.

Monsieur Hortensius Guignonnet, who entitled himself, on his business cards, a "painter of history and graces" had been for ten years the most vicious dauber in Paris, running after young women, moving house every time the rent fell due and smearing horrible and indecent paintings, while swearing that nudes were his specialty.

Monsieur Guignonnet's studio was the rendezvous of all the worst among the pupils of our various masters: beer-drinkers, smokers of seasoned pipes and "lone cavaliers" of public dance-halls. The "lone cavalier" is a specialty much appreciated by the lovers of *barrière* choreography.

It was in one of those gardens, where the art of dance procured such great successes for Hortensius

Guignonnet's friends, that his admiration was immediately captivated by a prodigious *avant deux* executed in such an audacious fashion that Monsieur Guignonnet was bitten in the heart by the serpent of jealousy. But like the Italian painter, one of the predecessors of the great Guignonnet, who, about to lacerate the painting of a rival with his dagger in a fit of rage, threw his weapon away crying "Never—it's a masterpiece!" Hortensius suppressed his evil sentiment and, running to the executor of the marvelous step, held out his hand to him, saying: "You're good! If you'd care to teach me your solo, I'll give you my seasoned pipe and pay you six tankards or two absinthes, your choice..."

The bargain was accepted by the stranger; those two fine natures had understood one another, and that was how Monsieur Hortensius Guignonnet, painter of history and graces, became the friend of Monsieur Mimi Taloche, Henriette's brother.

Mimi Taloche and Hortensius were soon inseparable. The former was adored in the studio; he had wit, and Guignonnet found that he had a slightly roguish tone, which, he added, clashed with the high tone of the establishment, but made the messieurs laugh.

Friendship is sometimes imprudent, and Mimi Taloche learned that to his expense; he committed the fault of introducing to his friend Hortensius Mademoiselle Pervenche, known as the Ablette, so-called because of her alert manner, her wasp waist and her frilly clothes.

The Ablette was a model by profession, as her worthy mother had been; but the young woman's nature was better than that of the author of her days, and it was not without a great effort and long hesitations that she resolved to take up that strange profession. And even then, she brought to it numerous restrictions.

Thus, as the young gamin had said to me, the Ablette readily consented to allow her pretty shoulders—of a rare pallor and perfection—to be sketched or painted, but her concessions stopped there, and the distinguished painters before whom the child posed had always respected her scruples.

As for Mimi Taloche, who called her his mistress, he was lying odiously in saying so. The poor young woman, left to herself, neglected by her mother, having no aptitude for work, had met Henriette's brother in the course of her idling. Greedy and coquettish, the dainties he brought her and the little presents he gave her that he bought with his sister's money, ended up attaching her to him. But when he tried to obtain more than a few kisses and insignificant liberties, she went crimson with anger, and put him off until he was in a position to marry her.

Now we know how Mimi Taloche occupied himself in procuring a profession.

The strolls continued nevertheless.

"Cuckoos," those atrocious carriages in which an emaciated horse pulls a dozen passengers, were the usual conveyances of Mademoiselle Pervenche and her companions. It was in one of those rural peregrinations that the Ablette made the acquaintance of Monsieur Hortensius Guignonnet. The painter was in funds that day; he was dining under a dusty arbor in a tavern in Meudon.

At dessert, the seductive Hortensius took possession of the young woman's knee under the table and squeezed it very amorously, but a brisk and slender hand administered him the finest slap that he had ever received in his life.

"That's what you get for permitting yourself stupidities with my good friend," said Mimi, who had understood everything. "Oh, it's a proud virtue, that one, and you can see that it doesn't have a dead hand."

That occasioned a furious anger that the gallant painter did not allow to show, but he swore to avenge himself, and he kept his word.

"I've never encountered a model as savage," he said between gritted teeth.

"That's because she's not a model like any other," replied Mimi. "A model for the shoulders and that's all. The representation finishes there, the rest suppressed by superior order."

"It's because she's badly built, then," said Guignonnet, coarsely.

It would not have taken much for the Ablette's fingernails to reply to that insolence, but Mimi took charge of the response.

"I'll tell you the day after our wedding," he continued, "and if you have the misfortune to repeat that, by Lachincholle, my illustrious professor of kick-boxing, I'll pass my leg over you and squash your muzzle, as true as I'm breaking this glass, for which you'll pay the damages as it's you who's picking up the bill."

And so saying, he took the Ablette by the arm and quit the creator of the school of graces, who was foaming with rage and meditating his vengeance.

All that happened a week before the night full of emotions when the courageous gamin risked his life to recover the testament that Freyschutz had stolen.

Mimi Taloche, in spite of his promises and fine resolutions, did not go back to the house. After having gone to "smarten himself up," as he had written to me, in a clothing store, he had found himself so handsome in his new costume that he had been unable to resist the desire to go and show it to the Ablette

Armide kept Renaud, and they had undertaken an excursion to Meudon thanks to the few louis I had left in my purse.

One morning, when Mimi was waiting for the young model in a poor room that he had rented in the Faubourg Saint-Denis, he received the following letter:

My dear Toutou, don't expect me this morning. I'm at the studio of Monsieur Gallimard, a famous painter, who has asked for me to pose for three-hours at twenty francs the session. Come to meet me there; it's No. 20 Rue Pierre-Lescot.

"Number 20 Rue Pierre Lescot!" cried the young man. "But that's where Guignonnet lives, and I don't know any other painter in that house."

Then a thought came to his mind, doubtless so terrible that he launched himself downstairs and started running like a madman to reach the street indicated in the letter.

In the meantime, this is what was happening at Number 20 Rue Pierre Lescot.

An old gentleman with spectacles on his nose was sitting in the middle of a rather vast studio, in front of a table laden with fruits and succulent pastries.

Someone rang the doorbell lightly, and an old woman with a rather vicious face immediately went to open it.

"Monsieur Gallimard?" the Ablette asked the old woman.

"That's here, but Monsieur is having breakfast."

"I'm the model he asked for," said the young woman. "Mademoiselle Pervenche, known as the Ablette."

"Come in, come in!" cried the old gentleman, without quitting the table, "I'm expecting you. Damn, she's charming!" he continued, examining the visitor. "Sit down, my child. And I suppose, it's so early, that perhaps you haven't eaten?"

"I had my cup of milk this morning," said the Ablette, blushing, glancing from the corner of her eye at the beautiful fruits and delicacies that were covering the table.

"A cup of milk, nothing but that?" said the old gentleman. "That's not enough for a young stomach like yours. I'm not astonished to see you so thin and spare. It's necessary to nourish yourself, to nourish yourself solidly, my girl. Good nourishment fattens, it makes the flesh firm, gives bright colors to the cheeks, and it's with that diet that one makes beautiful models. Your shoulders appear to me to be round and plump, though, and I know you only pose for them."

"Yes, yes, Monsieur," the young woman hastened to say, "for them alone."

"Good, good, come closer to the table. Here are some nice cakes, some lovely peaches, and an excellent cream cheese." While speaking thus, the Amphityron served his guest, and encouraged her to do honor to his breakfast.

The Ablette did not fail in that. Reassured by her host's encouragements, she started pecking at a little of everything, like a sparrow loose in a wheat-barn.

"Now," said the old gentleman, take a glass, just one, of this Cyprus wine; it will go you good and give you strength. We're almost contemporaries, it and me, and we understand one another marvelously.

The young model drank the wine that was offered to her.

"It's very bitter," she said, stopping.

"It's an effect of age, my child. Old age has so much bitterness!"

115

The Ablette dared not hesitate any longer, and drained her glass.

XV. Psyche

Monsieur Gallimard continued talking to the young woman, but, as she listened, she experienced a disturbance, a vacuity, a confusion in her ideas that was augmented from one second to the next. In spite of her efforts of combat that strange condition, it seemed to her that all the furniture was spinning, that the dishes and plates were dancing on the table...that the old gentleman became a frightful monster ready to devour her.

And when she tried to repel those visions, muffled bursts of laughter were heard in a neighboring room; then the model's pupils became heavy, her eyes closed and she articulated, in an almost extinct voice:

"I believe I'm going to die..."

"No, no, my child," said Monsieur Gallimard, throwing away his wig and his spectacles. "You're going to sleep."

A few drops of laudanum in the wine offered to the Ablette had been sufficient to cause her drowsiness.

The charming gentleman who had committed that villainous action was one of Hortensius Guignonnet's friends, a former provincial actor. After having been whistled in all the cities where he had exercised his talent, the fellow had decided to divorce the dramatic art in order to devote himself to the art of painting; fortunately for him, no one whistles at painters.

"Messieurs," he said, as he went into the room where the master of the house was waiting with half a dozen of his honest companions, "I hope I played my role well?"

"Bravo!" cried the honorable society.

"That's the first time in your life that you've been applauded," added Guignonnet. "Now, to work! Prepare your pencils and brushes, Messieurs; I'm going to offer you a model such as Messieurs Gérard and Gros have never had.

"One moment," he continued, stopping a few of the artists who wanted to go into the studio. "Decency before all; Mère Bridoux, an old friend of mine whom bad politics have reduced to the estate of housekeeper, is charged with the Ablette's costume; she's going to make you an adorable Psyche. Let's have a glass of rum while the scenery is being changed."

"Psyche asleep!" cried one of the students. "Marvelous! It's Mimi Taloche who'll play Amour!"

That ingenious joke obtained a prodigious success; another bottle was emptied in honor of its witty author.

"It's done," said the horrible old woman, opening the door that Hortensius had closed. "The public may enter."

There was a cry of general admiration, which Guignonnet repressed with an imperious gesture.

The Ablette was lying on a chaise-longue, clad in a mythological costume and sleeping profoundly.

"To our easels, Messieurs," said the painter, "and silence now, or I'll throw the disturbers out."

The silence was not of long duration, for a frightful noise was heard. The entrance door was violently broken down, and Mimi Taloche hurtled into the studio. He saw everything and divined everything.

"You're a band of swine!" he cried "You've set some abominable trap for that young woman, for she wouldn't be here otherwise." He ran to her and shook her violently. "Let's go," he said, "and what are you doing here, wretch?"

"I'm sleeping," she replied, without emerging from her lethargy.

"They've made her drink some drug, that's certain," the young man continued. Then he seized the Ablette's garments and covered her with them.

"Now," he said, crimson with rage, addressing Guignonnet, "It's the two of us, you dirty rat, thief of young women, vile scoundrel. Come here so that I can spit in your filthy face, and then pop something for you—the eyes first and then the belly."

And, matching action to words, he "passed his leg" over the painter, as he had promised to do at the dinner in Meudon, and after having knocked him over on his back he rushed at his enemy with a savage fury and peppered him with kicks and punches, without it being possible for the other to get up.

The witnesses to the scene, momentarily nonplussed, precipitated themselves on the gamin in their turn in order to pull him away from his victim, but it was not without great effort that they succeeded in bringing Hortensius Guignonnet to his feet.

Agile and supple, as we know, Henriette's brother escaped from the hands of his adversaries, but he understood that it was about to be six against one, and that his fists, his natural weapons, would be insufficient for that unequal combat.

He examined the battlefield with a rapid glance and perceived a panoply of old weapons attached to the studio wall a few paces away. He then made a rapid retreat in that direction, walking backwards as far as the panoply; then, seizing an old saber that was within his reach, he turned swiftly toward his aggressors, placed himself in confrontation with them, and contained them by whirling his blade as the most skillful officer in the dragoons might have done.

In the meantime, however, one of the students slipped behind him. Profiting from his example, he took possession of all that remained of the old weapons: maces, battle-axes, saddle-pistols and ancient rapiers, and delivered the armful of terrible devices to his friends, who seized them.

Then they all fell upon the unfortunate child, who had wounded several of them with the point of his saber.

Their fury knew no bounds; they struck pitilessly until he fell, and would have killed him on the spot if their cries of fury, their oaths and the breaking of furniture upset in the struggle had not attracted the residents of the house, who, finding one man being struck by six others, tried to extract him from that horrible melee.

The worthy friends of the illustrious Guignonnet, and Guignonnet himself, seeing the studio filled with strangers, judged it prudent to execute a savant sortie. Those gentlemen therefore disappeared down a little service stairway, and when the agents of the police intervened, summoned by the honest Madame Bridoux, who wanted to hide behind the authority, they found no one in the studio but a wounded man who was covered in blood, his limbs broken, his head split, and the poor Ablette, who, under the effect of the opium, was still asleep.

An obliging neighbor had her transported home, and Henriette's brother, having been able to articulate my address, was therefore being transported to my house, where his unfortunate sister recognized him at the moment when he arrived.

A cruel scene of despair took place. Henriette, who had thrown herself upon her brother's body, clasped him in her arms, and did not perceive that she was drawing cries of agony from him by squeezing the young invalid's injured limbs.

"Come quickly, Monsieur Hubert," said Junon, running to the Chevalier's physician. "I've been sent to fetch you in all haste."

"Is it for the cat?" grumbled the doctor.

"No, no," said Junon, "it's for a human creature, although, you see, in the matter of the human creature, perhaps the cat himself..."

The doctor interrupted. "In sum, what is it?"

"A monsieur...a rather nasty monsieur, in parenthesis...whose head is split in two, his legs and arms broken, and you need to set fix all that."

"You're an old fool," said the doctor. "If everything were as you say, I wouldn't have anything to do in your house, and the patient would be dead..."

"But he's not much better," replied Junon, intending to justify her action.

"All right, all right," said the physician. "I'm coming."

A sad scene was offered to the doctor when he entered the room where the wounded man had been laid down.

Henriette dissolved in tears at the foot of the bed at every groan that her brother uttered.

Père Bonnefoi, pale and moist-eyed, was standing next to her.

I was supporting the head of the moribund in order to facilitate his respiration, which was ready to escape him.

As for Freyschutz, who had not quit Henriette since her return to the house, he was huddled in a corner, from which his gaze was glued to her—and that gaze, whose glare had softened singularly, expressed a profound sadness.

There are moments in life when the role of a physician takes on the imposing character of a priesthood. In the presence of an existence in danger, everyone tries to read in his eyes the verdict he is about to deliver. A father, a wife, a son, a sister, await with anxiety the words that are about to emerge from his lips.

Is it salvation? Is it death? Will science by the liberator or impotent? All thoughts, all hearts, reach out toward the man who is about to render you happy or reduce you to despair.

Silently, Dr. Hubert approached the patient. He examined him attentively, listened to his heart, his liver and his lungs, palpated his limbs delicately, and said: "The principal organs haven't been attacked; the limbs don't have any fractures; that's not where the danger is."

"Where is it, then?" I replied.

The doctor indicated the wounded man's head, and, taking me to one side, he said: "I might be able to save him, but there's a terrible operation to undertake, without delay: this very day, immediately. Will he support it? God alone knows."

"And if the operation isn't carried out?" I asked, trembling.

"He'll be dead in four hours."

"Don't hesitate, Monsieur," I replied. "If that young man dies, we'll have two deaths to deplore." And I pointed at Henriette, on her knees and praying by her brother's bedside.

"Come, Mademoiselle," I said to her. "The doctor wants to be alone with his patient."

She drew away, sobbing.

Then, addressing the mariner and me, the physician said: "As for you, Messieurs, you're men, and you'll help me hold the wounded man down." Then he took his case of surgical instruments, opened it, and took out a bizarre instrument, the sight of which made me shiver.

XVI. The Idiot

In the little garden of a house situated in the Boulevard Saint-Antoine, now the Boulevard Beaumarchais, the iron railings of which did not block the view of strollers, three persons were united on a beautiful October morning.

One of them, almost lying in one of those large rocking armchairs whose swaying provokes sleep, was Henriette Bineau, but so pale and so changed that one would have had difficulty recognizing her. Her pretty head was resting on a tapestry cushion, and her feet were enveloped in a soft blanket.

Père Bonnefoi, astride an iron chair, was smoking his pipe a short distance away from Henriette, who, in order to keep him close to her, had assured him that the tobacco did not inconvenience her, although a little dry and nervous cough when a cloud of smoke reached her, betrayed the affectionate lie.

The third person, a young man with thin features, almost bald, his haze fixed, atonal and bewildered, sitting on the ground a little further away from Henriette, seemed to be absorbed by an occupation whose object the other two individuals could not discover.

He was plucking the feathers from a poor sparrow, which was expressing its pain in little cries.

"What are you doing there, Mimi?" Henriette asked him, in a faint and sickly voice.

"I'm removing the feathers from a little bird to prevent it from flying. I need to amuse myself." And he displayed his half-plucked victim.

"That's frightful!" cried the mariner. "What would you say if someone tore out your hair like that?"

"Well, let them try," said the young torturer, angrily exhibiting redoubtable fingernails. "I've got claws, me, like Monsieur's big cat, and they'd see what I'd do."

"Oh!" said Henriette dolorously, hiding her face in her hands. "That's what he's become, though!"

The cruel operation that Dr. Hubert had carried out on the unfortunate had been a trepan—or, properly speaking, a trepanation, for the trepan is the instrument of which the operator makes us; it was a matter of removing a part of the cranium, literally staved in by blows of a mace, and also extracting a few splinters of bone that had penetrated into the soft part of the brain.

The dolors caused by the perforation made by the trepan are atrocious, and numerous cases have been presented in which the life of the patient has resisted but in which his reason has given way under the practitioner's surgical drill, however skilful the hand guiding it might have been.

Intelligence had therefore succumbed in the wounded man, but as the mud of troubled water rises to the surface, all the evil instincts of that wretched nature had flowed into the brain of the idiot. His vicious and malevolent penchants had taken on a bestial character; his extinct reason no longer being able to combat them, he surrendered to them with the absence of conscience of certain ferocious animals, which only seem to have been created in order to be hostile and harmful to humankind.

Two months had gone by since the events that had occurred in the Rue Pierre Lescot.

Henriette had been installed in her nice apartment, and the preceding scene took place in the garden of the house in which she lived.

I had persuaded Père Bonnefoi and his wife to come and live with us. The husband lived in my house; his wife never quit Henriette,

As for the poor idiot, I kept him away from his sister's sight as much as possible, and lodged him in my house, although his presence as very distressing for me. Henriette's delicate health had not been able to resist the frightful shock she had received; the sight of her brother renewed all her sadness, and Dr. Hubert recommended the greatest precaution.

I went every morning to obtain news of the invalid, who had become dearer to me by the day. As soon as I went out to go to see her, Freyschutz, who lay in wait for me, hastened to follow me, and went to press himself against the young woman, in search of a caress that she hastened to give him. Was that the affection that I testified to Henriette, or some other motive?

But the character of my uncle's cat, or perhaps that of my uncle-cat, had been singularly modified in my regard. He no longer avoided me, but appeared to seek me out and to be glad of my company. He spent long hours sitting beside me, following all my movements, and his eyes, full of intelligence, seemed to be searching my thoughts, divining their meaning, and sharing my various emotions.

Initially surprised by that change, it had ended up touching me; and the conviction that incessantly gained more strength within me of the transmutation of the Chevalier's soul into the body of his favorite inspired me with a keen and profound compassion for him. So, there were no generosities and attentions with which I did not surround him, and I then accomplished with devotion, and gladly, all the bizarre conditions of my uncle's testament.

It was, therefore, with a sharp distress and a profound anger that I witnessed the following scene:

I had just gone into the little garden, followed by Freyschutz, when the idiot perceived him and said: "That damned black cat again that comes to eat my dinner. Wait, wait, I'll serve you my dish, me." And, picking up a heavy pebble, he threw it at the head of the poor animal, which rolled on the ground, uttering a dolorous mewl.

"Little wretch!" I cried. "Were you only born for evil?" And I ran toward him, my hand raised to strike him; but he did not wait for me, and ran away through the garden gate, which was still open.

I made a sign to the worthy mariner, who followed him.

Henriette, very pale, put her hands together and implored me to spare her brother.

"He's barbaric, your brother," I said to her, beside myself

"Alas," she replied to me, stifling a sob, "he no longer has his reason."

I ran to Freyschutz, whom I took in my arms, and I searched for his wound. Fortunately, he only had a large contusion on the forehead, and when he opened his eyes again, he saw me kneeling beside him, gently rubbing his painful temple. I carried him to Henriette, and he looked at us with an expression that was so sad and also so grateful that two tears came to my eyes.

At that moment there was a dull growl behind us, and I perceived Fidele, who seemed very discontented with the caresses we were giving that new guest.

"There's another enemy for my poor Freyschutz, my dear Henriette; it's only you and I who love him here."

On the evening of that day, I thought that I was alone in my library when I suddenly felt a violent shock and a heavy mass weigh upon me.

I turned round swiftly, and saw to my great amazement Freyschutz, who had just jumped on to my shoulder, and was presenting me his head, as if to solicit further friction...

"All right, all right, I understand," I said to him. "This time, my hand alone won't be sufficiently efficacious," And, keeping him in the place he had chosen, I opened a bottle of a vulnerary substance. I poured a few drops on his forehead, and started rubbing it lightly.

Then, the most curious scene that could be seen was established between us.

A few scholars have claimed that there is a universal language in nature, which all the realms composing it understand mutually, and of which each possesses its dialect.

I can admit the elegant fiction of flowers in a flower-bed chatting between themselves by the light of the stars, or two nightingales talking about their amours, but, quite frankly, I cannot imagine two canaries or two pigeons asking one another for their news or making business deals.

I make an exception, however, in favor of the language of cats, one of the most emphatic that is known. The manifestation of their anger is similar to ours. Some of their accents resemble our oaths, and their tenderness is translated by passionate modulations that one does not find and does not hear in any other animal species.

The benevolent desire that I experienced to soothe Freyschutz's suffering doubtless gave my hand a magnetic power of which he felt the effects, for his gaze took on an expression so human that I was gradually subject to a strange hallucination.

The being placed before me disappeared, or, rather, his features gradually changed, and I then saw, distinctly, the face of the Chevalier de Saint-Harem...except that his eyes, the eyes of old, were no longer the same, and I could read therein a sympathy so true and so profound that I drew him toward me and pressed him to my heart, embracing him with a vivid emotion. And, prodigiously, it seemed to me that he returned my caresses and my kisses.

Oh, never in his first existence had he given me such pleasure!

"My uncle, my dear uncle," I exclaimed, in a transport of joy of which I was not the master, "may the overflow of my sentiments for you soften the frightful torture that you're enduring. God is my witness that I would give my life to render to you the person you have lost, but you have left me a sacred duty to fulfill. Your daughter, your Henriette, will be my wife, and we'll surround you with all the cares of the most serious affection!"

My uncle attached his gaze to mine, stretched out his paw along my arm as if to summon my attention, and I truly believed that he was about to speak to me, when the silence of the night was disturbed by a horrible scream, a cry of anguish, dolor and despair; and Juno appeared in my room, pale and scarcely able to stand, saying: "Come, come quickly! The wretch is murdering her!"

"My God, who?" I cried.

"Come, come," she replied, "you can't be too soon."

I launched myself on the heels of Junon, and this is the frightful thing I beheld:

In a large room on the ground floor of the house, which ordinarily served as the servants' parlor, a man was holding a woman by the hair, dragging her with one hand into every corner of the room, and seeking with the other to grab her neck in order to strangle her.

The unfortunate woman was making extreme efforts to escape the torture that threatened her, but the assassin succeeded in sliding his fingers under his victim's thick hair, making her feel their frightful pressure, and the unfortunate woman's groans were stopped in her throat, which no longer allowed anything to emerge but inarticulate sounds.

As I ran toward him, another man hurled himself upon the assassin, through a second door to the room, seized him with a vigorous arm, and threw him down on the tiles.

I ran to the woman, almost stifled, scarcely giving any sign of life, and carried her to a chair. Rapidly, I parted the hair that was concealing her face, and examined it attentively.

I had never seen her before.

XVII. The Ablette

The day after the terrible scene that had happened during the night in the Hôtel Saint-Harem, Père Bonnefoi and his wife were chatting in low voices in the small drawing-room that preceded Henriette's bedroom.

"There you are, finally!" the woman said to her husband. "But in the name of Heaven, where are you coming from like that? It's nine o'clock in the evening and I haven't seen you all day."

"Quietly, wife, speak quietly! It's necessary that Mademoiselle Henriette doesn't know a word of what I'm going to tell you."

The old woman got up, opened the door of Henriette's bedroom cautiously, and came back to her husband. "She's sleep," she said. "I'm listening."

"Her little wretch of brother kicked up a fine fuss yesterday evening," the mariner began. "A little more and he'd be marching straight to the Place de Grève. He's a scoundrel, that idiot!

"Can you imagine that the rogue had a mistress, an artists' model, the creature for whom he was beaten, in the home of the painter who got six months in prison for it? It was only this morning, when she recovered consciousness, that she told us what had happened.

"For two months she's been searching for her lover in every corner of Paris. Yesterday, when he ran out of the garden, she recognized him, and followed him back to the house, but she didn't dare come into it in broad daylight.

"'I'd found him so changed,' she told us, 'that I wouldn't go home without having news of him.' These little sluts," the mariner added, "fall in love like honest girls."

"When night fell, she slipped through door left ajar into the house and hid in a little glazed cupboard, determined to stay there until she was able to see Mimi Taloche.

"At about eight o'clock in the evening, my rogue came to sit in the servants' parlor as usual, and started building houses of cards; he likes that, the imbecile.

"Suddenly, the little one emerged from hr hiding place and appeared before him.

"He looked at her for a long time without recognizing her. Then his memory came back. 'It's you!' he cried, running to her. 'You're the Ablette, aren't you?'

"'Yes,' she said, "it's me, who still loves you, although you're no longer handsome at all.'

'Oh, it's you, wretch, who let yourself get dressed in I don't know what in the home of that gallows-bird Guignonnet; it's you who were about to be painted in that costume! You're a slut!' he went on, and his eyes were popping out of his head. 'Wait, wait, I remember; the bandits beat me; they smashed my head, and it still hurts...' And in the midst of his anger, his tears flowed... 'Then they stamped on me, the damned students, they thumped me, and I can still hear the painter saying to me: 'There, that's the slap your princess gave me, and this one's for you...they were six against one, my limbs were cracking under their boots and my brain came out of its box...and it's you who are the cause of all that! But I'll get my revenge; I'm going to give you all the blows they gave me...oh, how stupid I am; when I've thrashed you, you'll start again, and the others will beat me up. No, no, I have an idea...I'll kill you...that way, I'll be sure of you...'

"'Mimi,' she said, falling to her knees, 'don't kill me, my Mimi. I beg you...my old mother, who only lives on my sittings, will starve to death, the poor old woman.'

"'But he wasn't listening to me!' she said,

"'How shall I kill her?' he said, talking to himself. 'If I had a knife...but not even a clasp-knife...oh well, a bit of rope...I'll pay twenty sous for a bit of rope to strangle her.'

"'He tried to grab me, I got away; I couldn't see, I couldn't find the door again, I bumped into all the furniture...my legs would no longer carry me; I huddled in a corner, no longer able to move...and he was in front of me, with blood in his eyes and foaming at the mouth, heaping me with insults. Then he threw himself on me, grabbed me by the hair; I screamed...after that, I didn't see any more... I thought that I was still struggling, though...but I soon ran out of air...something squeezed my neck...I was choking...'"

At these words from the mariner, Henriette's bedroom door suddenly opened; she appeared on the threshold, and cried with an accent impossible to describe: "Is she dead? Tell me, is she dead?"

Immobilized by the sight, the mariner and his wife only ran to her when they saw that she was about to collapse.

"Animal that I am," said Bonnefoi, supporting her, "it's my fault; I started talking aloud without perceiving it." Addressing Henriette he added: "No, Mamzelle, she isn't dead...but if I hadn't been smoking my mouthburner in the courtyard, it would have been all over for the poor child, for I arrived just as Monsieur your brother's fingers were in the process of serving as her last cravat."

"A murderer! My brother, a murderer!" said Henriette, horrified.

A violent crisis of nerves took possession of her.

I came running immediately, alerted by Père Bonnefoi, and hastened to reassure her regarding the consequences of the young idiot's dementia.

Two months went by.

The poor Ablette had been taken by me to one of the best sanitaria in Paris, to which I had recommended her urgently, but she disappeared from the house one day without anyone being able to find her again.

As for the amiable fanatic for whom my affection for Henriette had imposed the responsibility on me, we locked him in a small building annexed to my house, and I confided him to the skill of Dr. Hubert.

A savant alienist, he first bled him abundantly and then, by means of graduated cold showers, succeeded in calming his furious excitement. His transports eased; a kind of mental and physical annihilation succeeded them. The idiotism regained the upper hand, and he was soon nothing but an inert and passive creature, of whom a child could have rendered himself master, so much had the poor, emaciated, etiolated body lost its strength and energy.

All those moving disturbances of my life had not distracted me from my affection for Freyschutz. Every evening, I found him in my room, running toward me and expressing his joy at my return.

Conversation, as can be imagined, was difficult between us, but even though I could not speak his language, I was certain that he could understand mine. His eyes responded to me, and their former gleam reappeared, to my great terror, when he experienced indignation or anger.

He followed me very assiduously to Henriette's house; she welcomed him with an intense pleasure. But the young woman's old friend, her dear Fidele, did not experience the same satisfaction as his mistress in Freyschutz's visits. He growled dully at the sight of him, seemed jealous of the caresses given to his rival, and left the room as soon as the latter appeared.

Those symptoms of hatred ought to have enlightened me, by reminding me of the mutual antipathy of the two species, but I did not attach any importance to it—and that was a grave mistake, of which I repented subsequently.

One evening, when the interesting invalid and I were alone, I noticed sadness and embarrassment in her features.

"What's the matter?" I asked her. "Are you suffering more, or are you hiding a chagrin from me?"

"You've divined it," she said, extending her hand to me. "My heart has been suffering for more than a month, even more than my paltry person, and I love you too much to keep silent about the reason. There is nearby, a few paces from this house, a poor being that I'd like to see again. I find myself cruel for having abandoned him for such a long time, and as I can't go to him, I'd like to beg you to bring him to me."

"My dear child," I said, "it's out of affection for you that I haven't done it already. The sight of him is so poignant that I feared causing you a dolorous impression."

"No, no," she replied, "I'm prepared for anything, but I want to see him again and embrace him."

"He won't recognize you," I told her.

"It doesn't matter. I'll recognize him, whatever ravages the malady has inflicted on him."

The next day, I brought her brother to her. He really was no more than a shadow of the person she had loved so much. But before introducing him into Henriette's room I demanded that she take a few drops of a potion that the physician had prescribed, and of which he had recommended that the invalid only be given very small doses, the elements making up the medication leading to grave accidents and even death if they were absorbed in too large a quantity.

The idiot came in.

I placed him beside the bed on which Henriette was lying and I said to him: "This is the person who raised you, who has always been good to you; look at her closely...recall your memories...don't you love your sister?"

"Sister...sister...," he said, pressing his forehead. "Sister... whose...?"

"Yours, yours, my poor Auguste!" And she opened her arms to him.

He drew closer to her, and gazed at her with a profound attention. It was evident that his memory was delivering itself to a difficult labor. Then, suddenly, enlightenment dawned; he uttered a cry of joy, and, seizing the young woman's head, he covered it with kisses.

But the emotion was too strong for the invalid. I saw her eyes close, her head tilt; I feared one of the spasms she experienced so frequently, and I ran into the next room in order to call for Mère Bonnefoi, who watched over her day and night.

The light of reason that had just sprung forth in the idiot was not extinct.

"She...she's suffering," he said. "Drink... drink... like me... relief... cure..."

And seizing the phial that contained the dangerous potion, he poured all of it into Henriette's cup, and held it out to her.

Having only experienced a temporary disturbance, she took the cup that her brother gave her mechanically, put it to her lips, and started drinking its contents.

XVIII. Dog and Cat

Only an unexpected occurrence saved Henriette from the danger she was in.

Two seconds more, and she would have drunk the fatal beverage, when Freyschutz, who had missed nothing of the preceding scene from the armchair in which he was curled up, launched himself on to the invalid's bed and tipped over the liquid that she was holding in her hand.

I came back in at that moment and I understood, on seeing the empty phial, the peril that my young friend had just escaped.

But the idiot screeched, pointing at Freyschutz: "Wretched, villainous cat; he's preventing little sister from being cured by the good drug that he's spilled."

In the meantime, Freyschutz had placed his paw on the physician's prescription, and was looking at me with a significant expression.

Thus, the Chevalier de Saint-Harem was evidently watching over his daughter, and his paternal soul had inspired him with the thought of using his new form to snatch Henriette from death.

As soon as I was able to tell her about the service that Freyschutz had just rendered her, he became her dearest favorite. Poor Fidele was neglected; even his mistress' bedroom door was prohibited to him, for, as soon as he perceived his rival, he barked with so much fury, and looked at him in such a menacing fashion, that the civil war in question caused the invalid emotions that it was necessary for her to avoid at all costs.

One evening, when Henriette, Freyschutz and I were together in my cousin's drawing room, forming, unknown to Henriette, a family assembly, I was seized by an irresistible desire to open my heart to the woman who was to be my wife, the confidant of my most intimate thoughts; to revealing to her the prodigious discovery that I had made, to initiate her into the struggle of my common sense against the evidence of a fact that it was no longer possible for me to doubt. And I thought that if I brought Henriette to share my conviction, I would feel myself relieved of the weight of a secret that I no longer had the strength to keep to myself alone.

"My dear Henriette," I said to her, "God knows that I don't want to attack your religious sentiments, but can you believe that among the punishments and rewards that are destined for us after our death. Heaven might grant us another chance to avoid the former or merit the latter?"

"I don't understand what you mean," she said, very surprised.

"For example," I continued, "if, after a first life, our souls changed prison, if they occupied in turn several terrestrial envelopes. Some, antipathetic to our former condition, would become an expiation of our past sins; others, in the contrary circumstance, would be the anticipated reward of our virtuous actions down here."

Henriette was gentle, sensible and loving, but her neglected education did not allow her to grasp the range of my words. Her intelligence did not have the elevation of her heat,

I became more precise.

"Suppose," I continued, "that the soul of a person that you might have loved tenderly were condemned to suffer the ordeal of another existence; and, after having been honored, welcomed and sought after in a first life, were forced to animate a primitive, perhaps bestial body, and you found in that wretched form the object of one of our most tender affections?"

"What are you saying?" she exclaimed, fearfully. "Don't talk to me like that, you'll render me mad."

"And if that creature," I added, "were there, close to you, incessantly by your side..."

"I'd die of terror," she said, faintly, "and I wouldn't be able to support the sight of such a being."

A shrill mewl, or rather, a cry of pain, resounded almost at my side, and Freyschutz launched himself with a rapid bound up to the casement of the room, went through it nimbly, and disappeared, fleeing over the neighboring rooftops.

"Oh my God!" said Henriette. "Is it Freyschutz that you were talking about?"

I saw such a distress on her features that I dared not confirm it, and contented myself with saying that I was talking about a theory by which the Chevalier de Saint-Harem had been impassioned, that he had brought me up in that singular belief, and that I begged her not to be astonished if those singular ideas sometimes returned to me in her presence.

For some days I had been experiencing a rather sharp anxiety; Fidele had run away from his mistress' home. Henriette, almost bedridden, often asked about him, but did not see him for the reason mentioned above. I had asked the mariner's wife to conceal the barbet's flight, but I was very troubled nevertheless by his disappearance. I had searched for him everywhere, in vain.

The worthy Bonnefoi had set out on campaign and had traveled the entire quarter without success. Promises of a reward, numerous posters—nothing had been able to put us on the fugitive's trail.

The poor animal had doubtless been unable to bear his disgrace, and the preference that everyone accorded to Freyschutz.

After his abrupt departure, the latter had stopped on the crest of a roof, from which he was able to see his daughter's lighted window. Everything that that soul had suffered since its cruel transmutation could not compare with the dolor it must have felt on hearing Henriette's last words, words so full of horror and disgust for its present nature.

I divined its chagrin, and ardently desired to see my unfortunate uncle again in order to soften the frightful blow he had just received by means of the evidence of my affection.

Alas, that last wish was not to be granted.

Some hours before, while I was spending the evening next to my dear invalid, the old barbet had returned to the Hôtel Saint-Harem—but good God, in what a state! Thin and emaciated, with a miserable rope around his neck that the person who had found him had doubtless used to keep him prisoner.

The efforts and the teeth of the captive had succeeded in breaking his bonds, and it was in that deplorable condition that the fugitive came to ask me for shelter.

The first person that he met in the courtyard of the house as the idiot, who, while nibbling a few pastries that he had stolen from the parlor in Junon's absence, was amusing himself with his usual malevolent instinct in destroying all the flowers in the house's small flower-bed and then trampling them underfoot, laughing in a stupid and sinister fashion.

"Hey! There's the big drowned thing!" he said, on seeing the barbet.

Fidele responded to that greeting with a growl of bad augury. Then, perceiving the leftovers of my meal, which the idiot had set down on stone bench while he was shredding my roses and carnations, he ran to that pittance and started devouring them gluttonously.

The idiot tried to snatch them away, but too late; everything had disappeared.

Furious at the barbet's action Auguste Mimi Taloche showed him his fist and raised the stick that he was holding in his hand. But the dog struck a defensive pose, and was about to hurl himself upon his adversary when the arrival of a new individual suddenly changed the scene and gave it a much more frightening aspect.

That newcomer was poor Freyschutz, who, after having run over all the rooftops separating Henriette's house from mine, had arrived at that of the town house, which he doubtless recognized from having so cleverly measured it on the night when he carried away Monsieur de Saint-Harem's testament.

With his customary agility, Freyschutz had descended on to a low wall that served to enclose the house. With one bound he was in the courtyard, and found himself in the presence of his redoubtable enemy.

The soul of the Chevalier de Saint-Harem showed itself entirely in that encounter, of which it scarcely understood the dangers.

Motionless before the big dog, launching the most terrible gaze at him, the latter sensed to begin with the effect of the poignant and dolorous fascination that my uncle had exercised in his original form. Fidele could not support the penetrating radiance that the green eyes of Freyschutz darted at him. He inclined his huge head in order to avoid it; but when his rival took a step toward him, he approached him rapidly, his jaws agape, uncovering his redoubtable canines.

Courage does not exclude prudence, and Freyschutz abruptly took shelter beneath a wooden bench placed beside the perron.

Fidele ran at his enemy, knocked over with a thrust of his powerful muzzle the obstacle that separated them, then, extending his enormous paw, he let it fall upon his adversary's back, where it was buried in Freyschutz's thick fur.

Patience was not the Chevalier's favorite virtue; the pain he felt was sharp; his blood flowed, for the hound's claws had penetrated profoundly into the flesh. The attack made him aggressive; he riposted with a thrust of his claws which attained one of the hound's eyes, and caused him such agony that the latter's anger became rage.

Then commenced the most furious battle that one could ever see.

In the meantime, the idiot, delighted with that spectacle, excited the combatants with the shouts and whistles customary to Parisian gamins when they see two animals at grips, tearing into one another.

The battle was frightful, ferocious and frantic. The cat had skill on his side, the dog strength and size.

After bloody skirmishes, the combatants clashed again, and no longer drew back; their two interlaced bodies twisted and clung to one another furiously. Sometimes the weaker of the two was crushed beneath the body of the other; sometimes the other labored the flanks of his enemy with his steely claws.

And that horrible melee was accompanied by barks of rage and mewls of despair.

And the idiot was still laughing.

It was at that moment that I returned to the house. Seized by alarm, I was about to precipitate myself into the midst of the terrible conflict when it was concluded before my eyes without my being able to oppose myself to its dolorous outcome.

The barbet seized his rival by the throat, sank his terrible fangs into him, shook him for a few seconds, and hurled him against the wall of the courtyard.

I uttered a cry of horror, and ran to pick up the body of my unfortunate uncle.

XIX. A Soul in Torment

My uncle's second death undoubtedly afflicted me a great deal, but not as much as the first. That new death was his deliverance and his liberation.

The unworthy and miserable prison that enclosed everything that was purest in him, had just opened; the matter had become inert, the triumphant spirit was released from its ignoble bonds, and launched toward the ether, its fatherland.

Imagine a captive emerging from a noxious dungeon, transported to a high mountain where the air and the sunlight caress him and envelop him, one with its perfumed breezes, the other with its warm radiance, suddenly replacing mephitic obscurity. Such were the joys that seemed to me to be reserved for the Chevalier's soul, after the cruel ordeals that it had endured.

Did that soul draw mine with it into unknown worlds? I don't know; but what is certain is that, two hours after the death of Freyschutz, I found myself sitting in my uncle's large armchair, in his bedroom, which I had not entered since his death, from which terror had kept me away for such a long time.

The room was dark; I was not asleep; my eyes were wide open, and I witnessed a strange and magnificent spectacle

An immense azure horizon extended before me. The clouds were beneath my feet. Only harmonious sounds interrupted a silence so great and so complete that the beats of my heart resounded in space, where they found an echo.

Gradually, impalpable creatures and forms so indefinite that I cannot describe them troubled the limpidity of the void, like light vapors swirling in the midst of a pure sky.

My gaze, dazzled at first by that prodigious light, eventually adapted to it. Then, I saw those beings gradually take on a human appearance. Their bodies were surrounded by mists; their features were designed as if through a window of unpolished glass. They belonged to both sexes, but they passed before me so promptly that it was impossible for me to focus on any of them. Their movements of ascent and descent were so tumultuous that I can do no better than to compare them to the bubbles of air that play in a tube full of water, vigorously agitated.

One of the creatures paused for a few seconds beside me, enveloped me in its diaphanous shroud, and carried me away through the atmosphere.

Rapid as that course was through the medium of the ether, I had time to recognize my guide. The flamboyant radiance of two green eyes illuminated our progress through the obscure regions that we sometimes traversed. And that strange searchlight illuminated everything around us!

I remember that I spoke without a voice then. Sounds did not emerge from my lips when I thought I was articulating these words: "Where are you taking me, Uncle?"

The Chevalier's soul penetrated my thought, for a fresh and pure breath slid into my ear, and I grasped this response: "Wherever it pleases Heaven to subject me to a final proof."

My uncle's soul had become one of the wandering spirits with which the world is populated, and which sometimes wait for centuries for the new refuge that is destined for them.

While traversing the vast steppes of the sky, we were joined by a host of traveling souls that were coming from earth, where they had accomplished their mission. Thanks to the marvelous intuition that permitted me to understand them as they understood me merely by formulating our thoughts reciprocally, I was able to enter into a rapport with them and learn the secret of the existences they had traversed.

One of them had quit the body of an old miser, whose vice it repented of having excited.

"The beast," it said to me, employing the language of Sterne, who called matter thus, "was dry, gouty, ugly, ill-formed and dirty. I lived in that villainous abode for sixty years. As a child, it sold its dinner and stole the steward's bread—that amused me; it became a man and a money-lender; then we worked on a large scale. Every louis brought back ten; we set traps for the sons of families, for penniless coquettes and gallant demoiselles without protectors, but some had millionaire fathers, others well-heeled husbands and the residues of youth and beauty.

"Our clothes had holes, our hats were staved in, our shoes had no toes, our shirts were black and out hands were as black as our shirts; we were even sparing with the water of springs. Listen, a draught of water cost two sous. But we were colossally rich!

"One day, the beast was hungry; it was a matter of changing a louis to procure bread. A stack of a hundred louis would now only have ninety-nine. There was a terrible struggle the between avarice and the need for nourishment. Wanting nothing more than a change of residence, I urged the body to resist. What did it matter to me that it was suffering? My ethereal nature put me above all terrestrial appetites.

"It resisted for a long time; too long for it, for when it went out into the street and went to the exchange to obtain a hundred centimes for its gold piece—gold being dear in that epoch—it fell, exhausted by starvation, on a street-corner. 'That old man's dying of hunger,' said a good woman passing by. Someone bought him I know not what coarse nourishment; he swallowed it with such avidity that, a few minutes later, he rendered his soul—which is to say that it gave me leave to go, and God knows, I've taken advantage of it."

Another spirit had just broken its tenancy with a ravishing woman whose good graces a ruddy-faced and fat Englishman had evaluated at a hundred thousand francs a year.

What ravished milord above all was her extreme pallor, which gave her the appearance of the heroine of a novel. That sentimental pallor came out of a pot of ceruse; now, everybody knows that the basis of ceruse is lead carbonate, a very dangerous substance rendered mortal by abuse. But as the paler the Englishman's mistress was, the more he heaped her with presents, the heroine of the novel renewed the layers of her make-up so often that one day she simply poisoned herself, to the great despair of her perfumer.

Then too, there was the soul of a gambler who had hanged himself for having too blindly followed a streak on red. There were also the souls of scholars whom a noble labor devoid of profit had worn away all the springs of their intelligent nature. And finally, there were the souls of poor little creatures who had never had any bed but a cradle. Those souls were the good Lord's angels.

And we were still traveling; we were soaring over all the peoples of the world, and we did not pause anywhere.

For a second time I felt the light breath of the Chevalier's soul, and I heard the words: "It's here!"

Then we descended gently toward the earth. At first, everything appeared to me to be confused; a thousand colors dazzled me: the emerald of meadows, the lapis of waters, the ocher of labored fields; I only distinguished a checkerboard in which each square had its different shade, or rather, a vast mosaic in which a divine lapidary had brought together all the precious stones in the universe.

Our aerial flight soon stopped above a splendid palace whose towers and dome threatened the sky. That palace was situated in the middle of a great city: monuments, temples, columns and statues everywhere. Those of the sovereign were in every square in the city, in stone, in bronze, in marble, on foot and on horseback.

"How this sovereign's people must love him!" I said

And my uncle's soul, diving my thought, replied: "They fear him."

We went into the King's palace. The greatest disturbance reigned there; his tearful friends surrounded a splendid bed on which the Prince lay dying.

The members of his family were weeping; his numerous generals, his ministers and his courtiers were putting on a semblance of weeping. The lord chancellor of the kingdom was preparing the funeral oration of the future deceased; he said very little therein about the virtue of the moribund, but he exalted those of his successor.

The soldiers were saying to one another: "A new coronation will obtain us a supplement to our pay." Schoolboys were rejoicing in thinking that they would obtain an extra day's vacation.

"The soul of that man is about to quit him," the Chevalier told me, indicating the dying man to me. "Soon, nothing will remain of him but a vulgar envelope that the earth will reclaim, if no other soul substitutes itself or his and replaces it. But there's a great deal of competition; all evil spirits want to be kings, in the fashion of Louis XI, Charles IX or Nero. Me, I shall be Titus!"

At that moment, a pale light that I saw shining on the forehead of the Prince was extinguished, but as the Chevalier's soul was about to launch itself toward the royal remains, another soul, swifter and more agile than his, took possession of it.

"What is that soul?" I asked my uncle.

"The soul of a brigand who died on the scaffold," he replied.

So the reign of that King was one of the most infamous of that century; he made an odious war, heaped his enemies with unprecedented exactions, despoiled them of their territory and covered the conquered soil with crimes of every sort.

"*Au revoir*," added my uncle's soul. "I'm going to look for a better domicile."

Obscurity surrounded us again; it seemed to me that I fell from an enormous height, and I found myself back in the Chevalier's armchair, with cold sweat on my brow, and trembling with terror.

XX. The Marriage

The impression that that vision caused me was profound, and cast a violent trouble into my mind, for I had the conviction that it was not entirely a dream.

But what was it, then?

Had I really seen those unknown worlds?

Had I been in communication with their strange inhabitants?

Would I one day live among them, and submit to some dolorous and perhaps miserable metamorphosis at the emergence from my present existence?

That evening, after having quit Henriette, I came back to sit on my own in the little flower-bed, the theater of the combat and death of Freyschutz. I had had his mortal remains buried under a clump of flowers, and there, during the early hours of the night, I passed over in my memory all the bizarre events of my life since the Chevalier's death.

Sometimes, I sensed that I was superior to other mortals by virtue of the discovery that I had made and the revelations that I had had; but more frequently, I recommenced in my mind the interminable struggle of my certainties against my reason, of the truth against the implausible; I argued with myself, and all that concluded with a complete annihilation of my intelligence.

What had been most painful of all in my strange existence was the cruel necessity of conserving for myself alone the frightful secret that I had discovered. Once, as you will remember, I wanted to confide it to Henriette, but the terror she felt at my initial confessions forced me to interrupt them and to renounce it forever.

One day, I had the idea of revealing everything to Dr. Hubert. He was an educated man, devoid of prejudice, whose honest mind and common sense were held in high esteem. I went to find him and told him my singular story.

During my long account, his gaze seemed to be studying my physiognomy; two or three times I saw the expression in his eyes of a great sadness, which I attributed to his sympathy for the misfortunes of the Chevalier de Saint-Harem.

While listening to me, without losing sight of me, the doctor seemed to be plunged in a serious meditation, but he did not interrupt me once, or make any observation, not seeking for a moment to combat my ideas, and did not appear to be surprised by anything I told him.

And when I asked him anxiously for his opinion of what he had just heard, he replied in a grave and slightly emotional voice: "Human existence is surrounded by mysteries that science will never discover. To want to penetrate them is above our strength and our intelligence; there is even a danger," he added, emphasizing the word, "in concentrating one's thoughts on the nature of what you've just told me, and you'd act sagely in seeking, in distractions or in study, forgetfulness of what preoccupies you at the moment."

Then he talked about other things, of Henriette's health, the necessity of traveling with her as soon as I had married her.

"But her nature in so exhausted," he continued, "that the wellbeing she is enjoying is almost undermined by the abrupt transition from her past misfortunes and the privations she has endured. Then again, all the shocks that she has experienced have weakened her mental state singularly. If you want to conserve her," he said, as he shook my hand and took his leave of me, "preserve her from any violent emotion. She won't resist it."

My visit to the doctor was far from having satisfied me; his response had been banal and evasive; he had seemed not to want to formulate any opinion of his own on the questions that I had submitted to him, and I regretted having opened myself up to him—for from that moment on I incessantly found in his eyes the cold and almost inquisitorial gaze that he had incessantly directed at me during my moving narrative.

We were at the beginning of November, in the epoch when nature gets ready to put on her sad winter dress, but the last days of which a mild and pale sun comes to illuminate, like the supreme smile of a young woman whom Heaven awaits.

In spite of the doctor's ominous fears, Henriette's health began to recover. Only her eyesight had conserved a great weakness, and the doctor demanded that she shelter it under a thick veil, and sometimes even a bandage when she had to withstand too bright a light.

One morning, when the atmosphere was mild and everything invited a salutary walk, I gave Henriette the choice of the objective of our little excursion.

"I'd like to see the beautiful Jardin des Plantes again, so close to my former dwelling," she said, "where I went in order to breathe in the perfume of its beautiful exotic flowers in the brief moments of liberty that my daily labor left me."

Two hours later, leaning on my arm, the charming young woman was strolling through the pathways of the beautiful botanical park, and under the influenced of the vivifying air that she was breathing, I saw her reborn to life; her cheeks were colored, and her slightly stooped stance straightened, like the stem of a delicate plant curbed by a storm, that rises up strong and proud in the beneficent radiance of the sun.

We were sitting under a clump of green trees, completely isolated. Suddenly, Henriette took my hand and said to me: "My poor friend, I'm going to give you both a chagrin and perhaps a joy. I'm afflicted by the idea that my life won't be long, and that we'll soon be separated forever."

I was about to interrupt her, but she begged me to let her continue.

"I owe you everything," she said. "But for you I'd perhaps be dead at this moment, of dolor and poverty, for I hid from you the exhaustion of my strength and a discouragement of which I was no longer the mistress. But you came to me like a good angel. You made me a gentle and happy existence; but what I prefer to everything else is your tenderness. You know how dear you are to me, and I'm going to prove it to you once more by begging you to realize our dear projects of marriage, in spite of my suffering condition, in spite of this bandage, which I will perhaps have to wear for a long time yet.

"In sum," she added, with a dolorous emotion, "I want to die as your wife."

On hearing those words, I took her in my arms and clasped her to my heart.

"Don't lacerate my soul any more with your horrible dreads," I said. "You'll live for me, for me, who loves you passionately; the existence *à deux* that you're asking of me fills me with joy; and if I haven't begged you sooner to grant it to me, it was to spare your frail health, the object of my most tender preoccupations."

"No, no," she said, smiling. "I'm often weak against chagrin, but I shall be strong against joy."

After that conversation, I had only one thought: to unite myself as promptly as possible with that charming young woman.

It required a long month for that; that month seemed a century to me.

The doctor, who perhaps thought that the marriage would be a diversion from the ideas that I had communicated to him combined his efforts with mine, and we finally arrived at the moment so desired and so long awaited by Henriette and me. We obtained from the good curé of the Église Saint-Paul, our parish, that the ceremony would take place in the evening. I wanted to avoid, above all, the curiosity that Henriette's blindness could not fail to engender, and it was agreed that the marriage would be made simply, without invitation, with only our friends for witnesses.

Only the poor idiot made me anxious, for, to my great astonishment he had been having moments of lucidity for some time that we had not previously seen in him. It was doubtless by means of an indiscretion on the part of Junon that he surprised our secret, for on the very morning of our union he said to me: "Little sister is marrying you this evening; me, I'm at the wedding."

Now, I was not sufficiently sure of him to risk admitting him to the ceremony, and I confided him to the guard of Junon, very dissatisfied with that mission, which prevented her from accompanying us, and left her in the sole company of that difficult prisoner. It is true that his debility was extreme, and that if he conceived a malicious project, he no longer had the strength to execute it.

But Junon, wanting to simplify her task, locked the poor fellow in a little cell that I had had prepared for him, and where he had slept since his malady.

There's no danger, Junon said to herself, to reassure her conscience. *The windows are barred and when he's cried a little, the monsieur will fall asleep, and tomorrow he'll no longer think about it.*

Henriette had only wanted to accept her wedding-dress from me. Nothing was more touching than that beautiful creature, all clad in white, with her eyes covered by a black satin bandage. Even the priest was very emotional when we presented ourselves before him.

For witnesses to our marriage we only had Dr. Hubert, my uncle's old advocate, and our two dear friends, the mariner and his worthy wife.

The ancient church, hardly illuminated, and the solitary chapel where we were to be united forever, had a grave and solemn aspect that impressed me deeply. Then a memory suddenly came to mind.

It was in that same church, in that same chapel, that we had rendered the last duties to the Chevalier de Saint-Harem.

My imagination was so gripped by that funereal connection that after having guided my bride to the altar, I thought I saw the shadow of my uncle designed on one of the pillars of the temple at the moment when we received the nuptial blessing.

I overcame my terror, but my hand trembled as I offered it to Henriette after the ceremony, to guide her back to our carriage...

My young cousin had supported all the emotions of the evening well.

The doctor followed us to reassure himself as to the health of his patient; we were all gathered in Henriette's small drawing room when the door opened abruptly and Junon appeared. Her features in disarray and her garments in disorder, and came to fall at our feet.

"What's the matter?" I cried, my eyes fixed on Henriette, who was beginning to go pale. "What scene have you come to play here?"

"Oh, Monsieur," she said, putting her hands together, "it's not my fault, I locked him up well. The neighbors say that he cried for two hours...and just now, when I went into his room, I found him on the ground, stifled, suffocated, his mouth full of blood. He was dead!"

"Who?" said Henriette. "Who? Who are you talking about?"

I ran to the woman to prevent her from replying, but I did not arrive quickly enough to close her mouth, and she cried: "The idiot, the poor idiot...your brother!"

"My brother! My brother!" said Henriette, in despair—and lost consciousness.

XXI. The Last Apparition

The violent anger caused to Henriette's brother by the sequestration that Junon had inflicted on him during our marriage had led to his suffocation and death. That is what the doctor's expertise revealed to us.

Two days later that sad event, Bonnefoi and I followed the funeral cart that took the unfortunate fellow to his final dwelling.

That young man was inevitably avowed to misfortune, I said to myself. *His life was one long suffering, and his death was as cruel as his life. Is one only born, then, to suffer such a destiny, and is it not rather, as everything seems to prove to me, a first stage in this world...a first step toward Heaven.*

For the observer, the enchainment of events that the atheist calls fatality is the object of a curious and often dolorous study. Thus, the tenderness of Henriette for her young brother had not been able to preserve him from the cruel events that had overwhelmed him, and those events were perhaps about to take his sister to the tomb.

In fact, the days that followed the death of the poor madman caused us the gravest anxieties regarding the fate of Henriette. Mute, motionless, indifferent even to my cares, refusing all nourishment, only accepting from my hand the cordials prescribed by the doctor, I saw her weakness augment every day, and her tears never ceased to flow.

The faintest light caused her poignant dolors; she no longer took off the bandage that covered her eyes. I was thus deprived of the joy of searching there for the ex-

pression of a tenderness of which her soft voice no longer gave any evidence.

The physician did his best to reassure me.

"It is," he said, "a temporary state, the consequence
of the new dolor that she has experienced. Time will
gradually efface the impression, and while it acts upon
the morale, an intelligent medication will render vigor
and energy to that debilitated young body."

Only that hope sustained me, for I was suffering
horribly myself; I sensed my mind weakening sometimes to the point that my brain seemed completely empty. Then the most bizarre ideas took possession of me;
all my old fears returned to me.

I experienced, above all, an indescribable dread of
encountering the soul of my uncle transmuted into another body. I felt myself shivering at the thought that the
Chevalier's terrible green eyes might appear to me un-
expectedly, and it was always with a sharp emotion that
I arrested my gaze on people that I was seeing for the
first time.

In spite of Dr. Hubert's anticipations, Henriette's
condition was getting visibly worse, and the worthy physician strove in vain to hide his sorrow from me; I had a
presentiment that the fatal moment as approaching.

Alas, that cruel presentiment was not mistaken.

Everyone knows how storms augment the suffering
of invalids, and are deadly to them.

One night, one of those frightful celestial cata-
clysms burst, in which lightning flashes succeed one another without interruption and the thunder seems to be
rolling from one pole to the other, when thunderbolts fall
and annihilate the dwellings of humans, and humans
themselves.

That night was frightful for Henriette; a violent agitation took possession of her. The silence that she had maintained obstinately for several days was succeeded by the feverish verbosity of delirium.

"This is what I dreaded," said the doctor, who scarcely quit her. "Tonight might annihilate the little strength that remains to her."

The name of her brother, mine, and that of her mother, emerged confusedly from the dear creature's lips.

"I feel ill, very ill," she said. "It's the end, yes, the end, of a sad life."

On hearing those words, my sobs burst forth, and I seized her hand, which I covered with kisses.

Henriette fell silent for a few moments.. Then, suddenly, she said: "Father! Father! Help me! Help me! I'm choking! I'm dying!"

Without noticing the strangeness of that appeal, I precipitated myself toward her, and clasped her to my heart; but Dr. Hubert thrust me away, abruptly.

"Go away! Go away!" he said, in an imperious voice. "Can't you see that she might die in your arms? It's air, air that's necessary. Get out, get out! I order it. The patient, at this critical moment, belongs to no one but a physician."

I went out, my heart devastated by dolor.

An hour went by, during which, with my ear stuck to Henriette's door, I tried to catch a word, a sound, a sigh; for my fate was being decided there.

Silence reigned in the room, but the thunder was still rumbling outside.

At the end of that hour of anguish, anxiety and hope, the door opened again.

The doctor reappeared. He was pale. His eyes were full of tears.

"Courage, my poor boy," he said to me. "It's all over."

I fell into his arms. I thought I was going to die too.

All my friends surrounded me; our dear physician, the worthy mariner, how wife and even Junon, who experienced a veritable affection for my young cousin. And all the sincere tears that were shed around me were joined by the lugubrious and dolorous howls of poor Fidele, who, like all his peers, according to legendary opinion, divined that death had entered the house.

It was with a great deal of difficulty that I was brought round.

I had fallen to a profound lethargy, which paralyzed my limbs, but without taking away the perception of my senses; for I did not lose the memory of my immense dolor.

As soon as I had recovered consciousness, my first thought was to run to Henriette.

The doctor stopped me.

"I forbid you that," he said. "You're not strong enough at the moment to support such a spectacle. This evening, later, I'll accompany you into that sad room myself, but I forbid you to enter it at the moment."

I pleaded and begged, but the doctor was inflexible.

"Listen," he said, making me sit down next to him, "you're sicker than you think. I've been observing you and studying you for me time with the experience of a physician and the heart of a friend, and I find in your mind an exaltation that frightens me, and I sometimes fear that your reason is going to escape you."

"May God hear you!" I replied. "Then I'd forget everything I've loved in this world and I'd no longer be suffering!"

The worthy wife of the mariner was charged with keeping vigil in the room of the dear departed. The doctor did not want to abandon me, and kept me company faithfully.

Toward evening, a singular phenomenon was produced in me. My tears dried up. I gradually felt reborn in my heart a calm that I had not savored for a long time. My misfortune appeared to me to be a dream that was about to vanish. I suddenly recovered confidence and hope.

I made the physician party to those new sensations. Far from appearing satisfied he looked at me with an expression full of compassion

"Poor friend," he said, taking me by the hand. He was about to continue, but I stood up resolutely.

"I want to see Henriette," I said. "I want to see her right now." And without giving him the time to oppose my project, I headed for the dead woman's room.

He followed me.

The old woman was on her knees, praying.

A candle was burning on the mantelpiece behind Henriette's bed.

I approached the mortuary bed. The curtains were partly closed. As I raised my hand to open them, my courage failed. I was seized by a glacial frisson; my legs buckled, and I would have collapsed if the doctor had not sustained me.

"You can see," he said, "that that cruel task is beyond your strength."

Without replying to him, I drew the curtain.

There was a movement on the bed, and I saw...what I saw...I scarcely dare believe it...I scarcely dare write it...

Henriette sat up slowly, her bandage still over her eyes, and extended her hand toward me, which sought mine...

"She's alive!" cried the doctor, beside himself. "She's alive! And yet, I was sure, perfectly sure that I saw her dead!

"But perhaps," he continued, in the greatest agitation, "it's only a momentary recovery of life...it's necessary to take possession of it at all costs... Ah! There...," he continued, "there, in the drawing room, that beverage, a marvelous elixir that I brought for an extreme circumstance. Perhaps it's this child's salvation!" And he launched himself into the next room.

In the meantime, I had seized the hand of my beloved and clasped it in mine, trembling that it might escape me.

But Henriette withdrew her hand swiftly and snatched off her bandage; and I then saw shining in the obscure alcove the two green eyes of the Chevalier. And a voice, which was no longer the voice of Henriette, but the ironic and mordant voice of my uncle, pronounced these words:

"I told you that we'd see one another again."

From that moment on, I no longer remember anything.[10]

---

[10] The feuilleton concludes this episode (on 5 August 1872) with a note advertizing the next episode, not for the next day, as usual, but for *après-demain* [the day after tomorrow]. In fact, there was a gap of two days, but the final episode, published on 8 August, was double the normal length. There

163

Epilogue

The story that you have just read stops with the last words of the preceding chapter, but the public wants a denouement, and will not forgive me for disinheriting it.

Now, these are the circumstances that revealed it to me; and, while hastening to give knowledge of them to my readers, I ought to declare that I am speaking henceforth on my own personal behalf, as well as what is written in certain legal documents.

Thus, I shall begin:

Some ten years ago, I was at the spa of ***, which is as renowned for the varied and picturesque locations in the midst of which it is placed as for the medical and powerful virtues of the waters. I admit that, like many enthusiasts, I was there more as a tourist than an invalid.

---

might be several explanations for that, but one of the possibilities, perhaps the likeliest, is that the author had intended to end the story at this point, but that the dissatisfied editor of the newspaper demanded the epilogue, giving him a day's grace to pen it, although he was then slightly late in delivering it. The first sentence of the epilogue might support this supposition, and if any reader should think it unlikely that a writer would end a story as brutally as the conclusion featured above, they only have to consult the endings of the three short stories in *The Terrible Nights*, especially "The Cottage in Zurich," to be assured that Henri de Saint-Georges was not at all shy of such brutality. The reader is therefore free to regard the epilogue as an artifice contrary to the author's original intention, and perhaps ought to do so. In the 1873 Dentu edition of the novel the epilogue is retained, but is retitled "Le docteur Hubert."

Having ingurgitated the regulation three glasses of water in the morning and taken the midday shower, there still remained long hours to employ, and there the difficulties of spa life began.

The country was beautiful, but the walks consisted of perpetual ascensions: it was necessary to climb, climb further, always to climb.

"You haven't visited the Eagle's Peak, the natives said to me. "It's splendid. From there you can see three rivers and seventeen steeples." The following day I went to discover the seventeen steeples and the three rivers.

"And the Deer's Leap? It's lost in the clouds and there's a hermit there who tells fortunes." Then there was the Serpents' Grotto, where I found nothing but frogs, and the Fays' Fountain, six hundred feet above sea level.

I was soon weary of exploring all those marvels in thirty-five degrees of heat, and I declared that I would henceforth be content to admire them in the *Traveler's Guide*. I abandoned the Alpine summits to the goats and the chamois for which Heaven had created them.

The meals at the host's table were very monotonous and very silent. I defied the most skillful talker to be able to "cackle his morsels," as Rabelais puts it. "May I offer you some wine? Will you accept a glass of water?" Those were the only phrases that were exchanged between people who were strangers to another, and who seemed to be accomplishing a chores in obeying the breakfast or dinner bell.

After a week of the mutism of a Charterhouse, I was seriously thinking of quitting that aquatic paradise when I found myself placed at table next to a charming young woman to whom I addressed some banal question or other, a poor fragment of conversation. She replied with a good grace that encouraged me.

"I can see," she said to me, "that Monsieur is as isolated as my husband and I are in this place"—and she indicated a handsome young man placed to her right.

We saluted one another and we started chatting about the locality, the sediment in the springs, and the marvelous cures that were attributed to them.

"As for me," the stranger said, "I'm very well; my wife alone has a slightly delicate chest, and it's for her that I'm here.

"Monsieur," he continued, as we got up from the table, "the traveler lost in the desert who encounters a compatriot experiences a joy similar to mine at this moment." Then he added, in pointing at the host's table: "There's the desert, and if you're agreeable sometimes to bring our two solitudes together, I'd be veritably charmed." He presented his visiting card, I offered him mine, and we separated.

The card that he had just handed to me bore the name *Monsieur de Mauriac*.

After that first skirmish of acquaintance, Monsieur de Mauriac and I often met up; I discovered new likeable qualities in him incessantly; he was easy-going, learned and modest. He had only one pride, that of possessing a charming wife, whose grace and kindness fully justified his admiration.

One evening, as I was walking alone under the long galleries of the bathing establishment by the silvery light of a magnificent moon, I perceived a man coming toward me.

"What luck," he said to me, as he approached me, "to encounter a client,, a friend, in this savage place; but I don't know whether I ought to offer you my hand, for, after all, you're in breach of regulations; you've come to take the waters without the permission of your physician."

"I've simply come to take the air, Doctor, for what I drink most is excellent Bordeaux, which costs me very dearly, and rather poor champagne, a near relative of the Normandy pear; but the champagne is a politeness of the host's table, and I return what I'm offered. But what brings you here?"

"My profession as a physician. I'm an inspector of springs, and every year I take a four-month holiday here; I've been on the circuit since your sojourn in the locale. Having arrived a few hours ago, your name was pronounced before me a few moments ago, and I immediately set forth in search of you."

"Who mentioned me, then?"

"Monsieur de Mauriac. I've just been to see his young wife, who is suffering slightly."

"A very distinguished man," I said, "of remarkable common sense and intelligence."

"Isn't he?" said the doctor, with an expression of pride that surprised me. "A straight and sure reason in all matters; a superior and solid intelligence. I'm proud of myself," he added, rubbing his hands.

"Oh, my dear doctor, you speak of that gentleman as an artist might speak of his work."

"Perhaps I have some right," he replied, "but not another word on that subject here."

An hour after that conversation we were in Dr. Hubert's little house, sitting before two cups of excellent tea.

"My dear client," he said to me. "I'm going to give you proof of confidence and esteem; the evenings are long at ***, the bathers go to bed early, and you Parisians scarcely appreciate that good habit. Our reading-room is poorly equipped, but I have, locked up in a drawer, a strange work that might perhaps aid you to get through your long evenings."

And he handed me a thick manuscript, in a hand-writing that was rather difficult to read; but the habit I have of mine, which is execrable, easily allowed me to divine the calligraphic hieroglyphs that covered the pages of the manuscript.

"Keep that entirely to yourself," the doctor said, "the secrets of physicians ought not to be made public; but I know that you sometimes dip into our science and that you're occupied with metaphysics; its thus under the title of colleague that I want to initiate you into the most singular case of my medical career."

I took the manuscript away and spent the night reading it.

The next day, I encountered the doctor.

"You haven't been to bed," he said. "I was sure of it."

"And what tells you that?"

"Your pallor and your fatigued eyes, certain indications of a sleepless night."

"It's true, in fact; your diagnosis isn't mistaken. And the end, doctor? Who will tell me the end of that bizarre tale?"

"Me," replied the old physician, "but know in advanced that it isn't a tale; it's a true story, whose consequences were dolorous for a long time. Spare me your impatience until this evening, and I promise to satisfy it."

That evening, at nine o'clock, when the curfew sounded for all the establishment's bored bathers, I went to the doctor's house, very anxious to hear what he had to tell me.

"There's no one as punctual as curious people," he said, laughing. "I'll begin. You've seen the role that I played in the strange events of which you've obtained acquaintance. I shall therefore continue the story at the place where the manuscript stops...

At the cry of horror uttered by Monsieur Albert Dumesnil in Henriette's room, I returned there precipitately, bringing the elixir that I destined for the invalid.

"Look! Look!" Albert said to me, in a paroxysm of fury, pointing at his cousin. "The eyes, *my uncle's terrible green eyes!* But this can't go on...those accursed eyes, which pursue me incessantly, which are making me lose my mind...I'd rather gouge them with my hands than be their victim again; I've suffered too much from them!"

And he launched himself toward the unfortunate child's bed in order to carry out his barbaric project.

I stopped him, and dragged him into the next room, where it required all my efforts and those of the old mariner to render ourselves master of him.

"But he's out of his mind!" exclaimed the latter, gripped by fear.

"I've known that for a long time," I told him, sadly, containing the poor fellow, who was trying to get away from us. Suddenly, he disengaged himself from our grip, pushed us away abruptly, ran to a window, opened it and as about to throw himself out.

The Herculean strength of the dock worker saved him; he hauled him back with his vigorous wrist and threw him down on a sofa, where he fainted.

I took advantage of that moment to part the lips of the unfortunate fellow and to trickle a few drops of laudanum into it, in order to paralyze his dangerous overexcitement.

The torpor was so profound that we were able to take him down to a carriage, which transported him to my house. I did not want him to recognize, when he came round, any of the places in which he had resided. I lodged him in a pavilion where I gave my consultations; it was surrounded by a large garden.

His lethargy lasted a few hours, and it was only by means of energetic frictions that I succeeded in putting an end to it.

I observed in silence the painful return of his ideas, and it was with a sharp anxiety that I saw the moment when he recovered his memory arrive; but as he began to interrogate me, I made a violent decision.

"Monsieur," I said to him, in a curt and harsh voice. "*You are mad!* And I am forced to treat you as such, for in your last fit of dementia, you nearly committed an abominable crime."

"I'm mad?" he replied, darting a terrible gaze at me.

"*You are mad!*" I replied, energetically. "And I am charged, as well as these messieurs, with keeping you out of sight and watching over you." And I showed him two surgical aides that I had summoned.

A horrible fever took possession of him, and lasted a fortnight. His excellent constitution saved him.

I carried out with that young man, of whom I was very fond, a bold medical treatment, breaking with the usual system of alienist physicians, which consists of diverting the thoughts of a madman from his folly.

For me, Albert Dumesnil was nothing but a monomaniac, and I wanted to extract him from his monomania by acting powerfully on his mentality, by convincing him that he had completely lost his reason.

A monomaniac enjoys the plenitude of his common sense with regard to everything except the object of his monomania; he speaks and acts then with great lucidity; but if his obsession returns to him, you will no longer find anything in him but a complete insanity.

I therefore treated my patient absolutely as if he possessed no light of reason. In our conversations I adopted a tone of pity for his condition that wounded him deeply…and the more I affected to feel sorry for him, the more he strove to prove to me that he enjoyed the common sense that I refused him. That was my aim; it was on that mental result that I had counted.

"Do madmen," he asked me one day, "conserve memory?"

"That's generally the first faculty that escapes them," I replied.

"That's good," he said. "I'll prove to you that I'm not mad."

From that moment on he wrote for several hours every night. What he wrote is what you have read. It is that singular story, in which natural and true facts are mingled and confused with all the chimeras and hallucinations of the monomania.

Under the long pressure of his uncle's Pythagorean reveries, he saw them, discovered them, and subjected all the actions of his life to them, attributing the simplest and most normal events to the obsession with which the innocent had been inoculated since childhood.

The memories that my patient retraced, far from overexciting his imagination, contributed to calming it.

"While writing down my impressions," he said to me, later, "I never ceased thinking about the madness with which I was thought to be afflicted. Calmer and more reflective, I asked myself at every page whether I ought not to give in to that opinion; whether the actions of my past existence did not justify it; and finally, whether"—and it was at this point that light began to dawn—"our souls, of a divine origin, could be resurfaced by their creator to the point of coming to animate abject and bestial natures.

"My weak intelligence had not been able to grasp that gripping and true thought sooner. The religious sentiments of my childhood gradually entered into my heart again, and I drew strength therefrom against my uncle's impious theories."

In spite of the evident amelioration that I remarked in Monsieur Dumesnil, I was not reassured as to its duration; I often found him sad and silent, and I caught glimpses of spasms of terror whose precise object I could not determine.

One evening, he went to sleep beside me. His sleep was agitated; incoherent words emerged from his lips. I listened carefully, and caught these words:

"Henriette! The alcove! The night! And *the eyes, the Chevalier's green eyes!*" He uttered a cry, and woke up with a start.

He saw me, took my hand and said: "Don't leave me…stay here, beside me. It's frightful! It's frightful!"

I calmed him down, but I did not ask him any questions; I had learned all that I wanted to know.

I divined that his will, that all his efforts, were struggling in vain against a terrible memory that he could not chase away. It required a violent means to rid his mind of one last chimera, and I prepared it.

One morning, when we were not alone in my study, I expressed my surprise that he never talked to me about Henriette.

At that name I saw him go pale, then he hid his face in his hands without replying to me.

"Have you no desire to see her again, then?" I continued.

"I dare not," he replied.

"Why? You loved her so much..."

"Why?" he said, with a feverish animation. "Because I'm a coward...because I shiver at the idea of rediscovering in her the voice and eyes of Monsieur de Saint-Harem, that horrible gaze that I saw on the cruel night when you thought she was dead!"

"What do you expect?" I replied. "Medicine has its errors...doesn't justice have its own? As for your cousin, you won't see that which you fear. She's blind."

"Blind!" he said, with a cry of color!

"Judge for yourself," I said, opening the door of the next room.

And Henriette came in, with her face veiled.

Albert ran to her, kissed her knees, and dissolved in tears.

But when he raised his head, Henriette had taken off her veil, and the softest eyes in the world brightened the most charming face.

"My eyes are no more changed than my heart, my poor Albert," she said to him, "And your sick brain made you see and hear what it heard and saw itself. But now..."

"Now, he said, hugging her in his arms, "happiness has cured me."

The doctor had just finished his story when someone knocked on the door.

"Come in," he shouted. Then he added: "The public is arriving a little late; the play is over!"

The visitor appeared.

"Pardon me, my dear friend," he said to the physician. "It's a hot night and I couldn't decide to go back inside. I saw the light in your window and I've come to finish my cigar with you."

"My dear client," my hoist said to me, indicating the newcomer, "may I introduce Monsieur Albert Dumesnil."

"Monsieur Albert Dumesnil!" I exclaimed, seeing before me Monsieur de Mauriac.

"I understand your surprise," said Monsieur de Mauriac. "The name is a pseudonym, a whim of my dear Henriette, for whom that of Dumesnil brings back sad memories. As for you, doctor, I ought to scold you"—and he indicated his manuscript, placed on the physician's desk. "I see that you've taken a confidant of my past misfortunes; but I forgive you." He extended his hand to me cheerfully, and said: "Don't worry, Monsieur, I'm no longer mad... except about my wife."

And the brave Fidele, who was waiting at the door, started barking to summon his master.

Note

In case the reader would like to know the fate of the other characters in the story, here is authentic information about them, of a powerful interest:

Juno, former honorary cordon-bleu, is only charged nowadays with Monsieur Fidele's cuisine, the latter having become very greedy in his old age.

Père Bonnefoi, elevated by Monsieur de Mauriac to the dignity of steward, only has the fault of wanting to teach his employer's young son, aged five, how one seasons a pipe.

The Ablette, having entered a small theater as a bit-part player, emerged therefrom as a Bavarian countess, by virtue of her virtues—and her pretty shoulders—and is now the very model of womanhood.

THE TERRIBLE NIGHTS

I have tried to be as cheerful as Jérôme
and as frightful as Rutwen.[11]
To People who have Nothing to Do

Idle reader, amiable subject of high society, when, after having tired out your horses in the morning, your stomach with a sumptuous dinner and your person in the evening, you return home at midnight, exhausted by pleasures, perhaps cursing in a whisper the mistress who is ruining you or the frivolities for which you are selling your lands, tell me: if there were a generous friend at your bedside who poured the balm of gaiety upon the wounds of your heart, or who, by means of a varied narrative, joyous or terrible, gave another direction to your

---

[11] The Jérôme cited is presumably the hero of the 1805 eponymous novel by Pigault-Lebrun (1753-1835), an irreverent author who was obviously one of the influences on Saint-Georges work, and whose preoccupation with the iniquities of forced marriage are frequent echoed by him. "Rutwen," more usually rendered Ruthwen in France, became famous in Paris in 1820 as the villain of an enormously successful stage adaptation of John Polidori's novelette "The Vampyre" (1819, widely misattributed at the time to Lord Byron), written by Achille de Jouffroy, with the assistance of Charles Nodier and Jean-Toussaint Merle—the theater's director—for the Théâtre de Porte-Saint-Martin in 1820, and quickly provided with a anonymous supplementary novel by Cyprien Bérard, widely misattributed to Nodier because he provided an introduction to it.

thoughts, would you not owe him some gratitude? Would your affable mind, a profound connoisseur of the amiable flatteries of society, not employ a few of them to thank your complaisant storyteller?

Well, that friend who dissipates chagrin, distracts from pleasure in order to render it keener afterwards, is my book.

If François or Lafleur, your supplier of literature, informed of the existence of my work by his friend, the chambermaid of a dancer, who received it from an ambassador—a partisan, like his mistress, of strong emotions—if your valet has placed it on your night-table, pick it up, and prove to the author your gratitude for the effect it has produced on you by disdaining to play Aristarchus[12] in its regard; leave the journalist the concern of judging it; and in the salons in which your amiability makes you an oracle, indicate this volume to unfortunate gamblers, jealous lovers and sensible women; if you buy it, your bookseller's press will often groan.

---

[12] The reference is to the pedantic 2nd-century grammarian Aristarchus of Samothrace, not the astronomer of the same name.

FELIX; or, THE CERNEY FAMILY

I. The Phantom

Bang bang!
Everyone is asleep...
Where is this?

Moderate your impatience, dear reader, and if you have no fear of imitating the people with whom I shall entertain you, continue and you shall see.

Old Dumont has just closed the main gate of the courtyard of the Château de Cerney, and is preparing to pay his tribute to Morpheus—or to speak without metaphors, to go to sleep—when several repeated blows are heard at the little door to the park, next to which his house was situated.

Dumont, the pearl of concierges for exactitude, politeness and fidelity, nevertheless cannot retain a coarse oath, extracted from him by the importunate knocker; but, immediately sacrificing his repose to his duty, he seizes in haste one of the garments he had just taken off, threads his thin legs into the sleeves of his coat, and, exchanging the employment of two parts of his garb, puts his fleshless arms into the legs of his trousers.

In that brilliant outfit, worthy in every respect of the hero of La Mancha, our concierge advances proudly toward the accursed door, at which someone is knocking incessantly. Suddenly, however, he stops, makes a list of the inhabitants of the château, and, believing that he recalls that none of them is out, he forces his hoarse voice and cries as loudly as possible the terrible: "Who goes there?" by which Parisian ears are so frequently deafened.

"It's me, Dumont; open up quickly, I'm numb with cold."

"Oh, it's you, Joseph; I thought you'd come back a long time ago, along with your young master. What the devil are you doing out at his hour?"

"What does it matter? Do I have to account to you for my actions? Are you charged with surveillance of the conduct of Monseigneur's servants? You have enough functions without adding that of my supervisor. Come on, you old fool, hurry up, if you don't want me to warm myself up at the expense of your shoulders."

"Gently, Monsieur Valet de Chambre, gently. Calm down, and know that no old soldier has ever allowed himself to be struck by a rascal of your sort."

After that heated response, our Argus finally decides to put the key in the lock; the door swings on its hinges, the concierge raises his head, and his eyes are immediately struck by the most frightful spectacle: a man, a devil, a giant, covered in a white shroud trailing all the way to the ground knocks him out of the way with a robust punch, and disappears, running at top speed toward the château.

At that sight, the frightened old man drops the lantern that has illuminated that scene of horror, and then, with a sudden turning movement, seeks to escape the lugubrious spectacle by flight. However, his tailor not having destined his coat to serve as a pair of trousers, has not given it the amplitude necessary to lend itself to the precipitate march of fast-moving legs, Dumont finds himself interrupted in his retreat and falls full length on to the ground. He utters a lamentable cry, which is repeated and multiplied by the echoes of the courtyard and those of the château.

Immediately, seigneurial heads appear at the widows of the building—oh, but heads of which you have no idea, my dear reader. To render the conclusion of my story clear, I shall translate before you the various persons whose sleep Dumont's fear has interrupted.

Picture, on the middle balcony of the first floor, an old man of sixty, of the most venerable exterior, with a face most appropriate to inspire respect; depict him in a night-shirt; placed beside him, Madame his wife, a small, thin, pale woman, seemingly very discontented to have been disturbed in the midst of a charming dream or an even more charming reality.

On the second floor, you can remark at the same window as her governess, an angel, an houri, a marvel—an object, in sum, about whom you will perhaps be as mad as I am, when you know her better: seventeen years old; blonde hair in the most seductive disorder; moist blue eyes, open but half-closed; a hand as white as yours, Madame, which is seeking to hide nascent treasures in pleats of jealous muslin. Such is Lucie, the daughter of the house and the sister of the young scatterbrain that you perceive on the fourth, in the mansard of that scoundrel Joseph, and who is laughing with all his might on seeing the spectacle that you have just witnessed.

But what do I glimpse up there? What is that formless group whose bizarrerie surprises and confounds the most subtle calculations made to define it?

Let us transport ourselves to the skylight from which those two mingled heads are emerging, and listen.

"What's happening, my dear Louise?"

"In truth, I have no idea, Pierre. I'm lost…my virtue…"

"Let's not talk about that; let's concentrate on the means of getting our heads out of this accursed window, into which too much precipitation caused us to put them, inconsiderately."

"Ah! Ah! You're twisting my neck!"

"Oof! Oof! I can't do any more; I'll die of it! Oh my God, I've just dropped my candle; what if it falls on Monsieur or Madame!"

Do not worry, amiable couple; it has fallen to one side.

"My dear Comtesse," says the Comte, on his balcony, "what's that?"

"It's a candle, my dear Comte."

"Hey! Pierre! Lafleur! Joseph! Come quickly."

All the valets arrive, and Monsieur de Cerney sends them to pick up Dumont, who is still lying in the middle of the courtyard where we have just seen him; and Lucie runs to investigate the cause of all the noise; and Felix goes into his mother's room, rubbing his eyes, which have never been so widely open; and Pierre, as well as his companion, who, on the point of choking, cried as loudly as their mutual embarrassment permitted them, fall silent.

In sum, all that fuss comes to an end, because everything comes to an end in this world, even the chapters of my story, and, the two patients having been freed by splitting the wooden frame with a hammer-blow, and Dumont having been rubbed over and over after his fall, everyone goes to bed thereafter—including me, reader, who wishes you a good night and no cowardly concierge.

II. On the Dangers of Admiration

How many people in society throw themselves head first into dangers or pleasures by virtue of stupidity, recklessness or passion? What happens so frequently in moral terms in society had just happened in physical terms at the Château de Cerney, on the famous night whose story you have just read, when an officious hammer delivered the compressed heads of Gros-Pierre and Louise, whom amour or the devil—which is almost the same thing—had brought together in Gros-Pierre's mansard, where the gallant gardener gave his nocturnal audiences to the facile beauties of the area. Jealousy had led Louise, the Comtesse's chambermaid, to carry out a search of her lover's room; idleness had retained her there; curiosity had sent her to the skylight, and the two guilty parties were sacked the next day for having sinned before the entire château, out of curiosity, idleness, etc.

Ten o'clock has chimed, and the bell has brought everyone together for breakfast when loud sobs are heard at the dining room door.

"Will Madame le Comtesse dismiss a poor girl who didn't think she was doing anything wrong in climbing up to a skylight to see what was happening in the courtyard?"

"Monsieur le Comte having promised to marry Louise and me," adds Pierre, "I thought that..."

"Throw those people out," says the old Comtesse, pretending to blush, "and never let them reappear before my daughter and me."

"But Mother," said Felix, "it seems to me that a good marriage..."

"Nothing ought to seem to you, Monsieur, and if your father consents to it..."

"I oppose, on the contrary," says the Comte de Cerney, severely, "the sacking of those two servants; if they are culpable, I shall offer them the opportunity to cease to be; I shall marry them and endow them; I shall promote Dumont to the position of steward and I shall make Pierre concierge, in order that, if ghosts conceive the desire to frighten him again, he can give them a sound beating. Well, Felix, what are you laughing at?"

"It's nothing, Father, just the funny face my sister pulled on hearing you talk about last night's ghost."

"Don't worry, Mademoiselle Lucie," said Pierre, "the phantom's shoulders will be as black as the devil's ears if I ever caress them."

At these words, Felix bursts out laughing in a manner so noisy that his mother, already furious at seeing Louise—whom she cannot suffer because she is young and pretty—remain in her employ, orders her son to leave the table.

Lucie, afflicted by her mother's rigor, sheds a tear and goes down to the garden; the Comte de Cerney gets up and leaves in order to go hunting; the Comtesse, who is due to dine at the home of the Marquis de Lavo, her neighbor, commences a toilette at eleven o'clock that will finish at five; and Felix runs to find his valet Joseph, whom he knows to be an utter good-for-nothing, but of whom he has need, as you shall soon see.

"We had a narrow escape yesterday evening," says the young man, on encountering the valet de chambre coming out of the cellar with his pockets garnished with two stolen bottles.

"My dear master," replies the drunkard, wiping his mouth, I warn you that I won't risk any longer accompanying you in your nocturnal excursions; there are too many dangers in playing the ghost in order to get home."

"Also, Monsieur Clown," says Felix, "it was necessary to find another expedient to get back to our room. Your unfortunate brain, ordinarily so fertile in roguish tricks, might have furnished you with a less singular entrance; but no, Monsieur takes advantage of the embarrassment we're in to play the role of phantom for me, hoisted on his shoulders, covered in the sheet that allowed us to quit the château by the aerial route; he thinks it funny to make an imbecile of a concierge die of fright, to wake up my father, my mother and my pretty sister. In truth, Joseph, it's necessary for me to be as good as I am to suffer all your stupidities and forgive you."

"Oh, no, Monsieur, oh no, it isn't goodness that preserves your confidence in me; it's the impotence you've have to get rid of me."

"Wretch!" cries Felix.

"Gently, my dear Master," adds the drunkard, "gently—let's think about it. You like women; when one is young and rich like you, that's quite natural; you found Mademoiselle Louise pretty; you charged me with informing her of it, and in consequence of the admiration she caused you, Mademoiselle Louise, whom you couldn't marry, has made advances to Gros-Pierre, and will become his wife. Such things often happen, so I find it quite natural; but what is far less so is that last Sunday, the daughter of the Marquis de Lavo, young Emma, while dancing with you at her father's house, caused you the same admiration as Mademoiselle Louise.

"As the heart of Mademoiselle de Lavo has never beaten for anyone, you took it into your head to look at her tenderly; you squeezed her hand, so white and pretty. Her old papa, who sees hardly anything, because of a rheumatism that causes firelight to cloud his eyes, did not perceive your disappearance from the drawing room with his daughter; as many people were strolling in the park to avoid the heat of the ballroom, you had persuaded the innocent Emma to imitate the strollers.

"While accompanying her, talking about the pleasure of dancing when one is fortunate enough to be the cavalier of a pretty girl, you had gradually withdrawn Mademoiselle de Lavo's white glove; you had caressed the delicate arm that you had just uncovered; each of her fingers had received the homage of your kisses; Mademoiselle Emma, who was unaccustomed to being thus embraced, began to blush very forcefully; a little temple presented itself, you proposed to the charming girl to go into it, in order to repose there.

"Modesty then broke the prism of innocence; Emma refused; your sudden flame, animated more than ever by her resistance, was unable to accommodate a refusal; your arm went around her pretty waist; your lips burned hers; your body sensed and savored all the parts of hers; her breasts were covered by your caresses; her eyes were closed by weakness and voluptuousness; no more ramparts for your hand...Emma is about to cease to be so pure...

"I appear; brought to that part of the garden by hazard, without intending to, I do a good deed in saving innocence; Emma, quicker than an arrow, escapes you, and the darkness and the foliage soon hide her from your eyes.

"Fate has rendered me master of your secret; hoping that I will be able to serve you, you revealed the adventure to me that I have just recounted in order to prove to you that I have not forgotten any of it. By virtue of my advice, we went out last night in order to seek to penetrate into Monsieur de Lavo's park and from the park into Mademoiselle Emma's room; but the old marquis' château is a good league from here; we weren't able to quit your room until ten o'clock in the evening; we didn't reach Monsieur de Lavo's courtyard until eleven, and two enormous dogs having immediately taken possession of the bottoms of our trousers, we promptly left them there and came back here to play the ghost, dampened by rain and sweat, bitten in one of the noble parts of our person, and no further forward than the night before.

"Believe me, Monsieur Felix, forget with good grace the petty sarcasm of a drunkard, and as you're necessary to me in order for me to be able to get drunk, just as I'm useful to you for my advice and my skill, let's live in peace, and be sure that, if Emma remains a maiden, you'll have done everything possible to preserve her from that misfortune."

That conversation had taken place in the cellars of the château, where Joseph was more often to be found than anywhere else. Felix, convinced by his passion of the soundness of the valet's argument, gave him a kick up the backside as a sign of amity, and ran to his room to make a very careful toilette, in order to complete the conquest of Mademoiselle de Lavo, in whose house he was due to dine with his family.

I can hear whips cracking, and a carriage entering the Marquis' courtyard; the door opens, and Felix is next to Emma.

III. Which is of Little Significance

They have left the table.

"Twenty-two points, Marquis. I've won. Would you like a rematch?"

"No thanks; I've been beaten enough for today, but in truth, you have an insolent luck."

"Luck! Oh, it pleases you to say so; when have you seen anyone win three games of billiards with luck? I have skill."

"But damn it," replied the Marquis de Lavo, "I haven't lost that which I had when, on my ship in harbor at Brest, ten years ago, I let the Prince de Conti win, out of politeness, the famous game of which the *Mercure de France* rendered such a detailed account. Oh, my friend," the old admiral added, delightedly, "if you'd seen the feast I gave the Prince, how content Monseigneur was, and above all, how amiable and attentive he was to my wife; he promised to hold my first child. I was twenty years older than my late wife; well, believe me, the Prince's promise rendered me so vigorous that, nine months later to the day, the Marquise de Lavo gave me my dear Emma; I called upon Monseigneur to keep his word and I was made...admiral."

At those words, the Comte de Cerney, in order not to burst out laughing in the face of the old Marquis, went back into the drawing room, where the Comtesse, who was doing some tapestry-work, and Lucie was accompanying on the piano a very tender duet sung by her brother and the sensitive Emma. The entrance of the two old men interrupted the young people, who followed their parents into the park. Felix gave one arm to his sister, the other to Mademoiselle de Lavo, and Lucie was incessantly obliged to warn her brother, who led her directly toward all the trees, so much had the force of his admiration for Emma been renewed.

There is no great harm in admiration, dear reader; the proof is that you, who are perhaps very moral—which is not proven, however, by the reading of this naughty book—must have very often admired a beautiful landscape, a precious item of furniture, a discourse on cheese by some orator who manufactures it, an improvisation on olive oil or Cognac by some other who sells it, the original nose and even more original wit of Monsieur P***, and a host of curiosities of various genres and substances. But what you might not know is that one can admire in several different ways, and that Felix was not admiring at all contemplatively the pretty arm that he was caressing and the rounded thigh against which he was pressing, under the pretext of an excessively narrow pathway, or that of a tree or a statue was getting in the way. Mademoiselle de Lavo was not duped by all those good reasons, but one is so weak when one is in love, and the senses are so new at sixteen years of age that one is not sorry to feel what one had not previously known to exist.

That should prove to you that I can talk morality and virtue as well as anyone else, when I take the trouble. I can plead innocent surprise, give sublime or touching advice, perhaps wring a tear from you by force of eloquence and falsity; but for every reader who likes to weep there are a hundred who like to laugh, and they will earn my bookseller more than the others.

"Damn, my dear Marquis," said the Comte de Cerney, "I believe it's raining."

"Heavens!" cried the Comtesse. "My butterfly bonnet will be ruined; in truth, Messieurs, you ought to have perceived the storm sooner, but no, when you're plunged in politics, you forget everything, including your wives. Comte, you are much changed with me." And while grumbling, the Comtesse ran ahead of all the society.

Her precipitation was harmful to her; for the sake of a drop of water that her coiffure might have received, she tore a superb amaranth dress of Tours plush and broke a fan that had belonged to Madame de Pompadour; and, what is worse, anger and humiliation caused her faint on the edge of pond, of which the salutary water was splashed over her face by the old mariner, who claimed to know all the virtues of that element thoroughly. Finally, when the Comtesse opened her eyes, she found herself lying in the bedroom of the late Marquise de Lavo, surrounded by witnesses to her misfortune...

That afflicted her more than anything else, for at a glance, she saw her cotton breast-pads and her false teeth on a table next to the bed.

It was too late for Monsieur de Cerney to return home. He was offered the guest bedroom, which usually served to accommodate an arsenal consisting of a rifle without a hammer, two rusty sabers and a pistol without a barrel. The beautiful Lucie was lodged in a little cabinet whose door did not close very well, next door to Emma's bedroom.

"Good night, goodnight, until tomorrow," say all the château's inhabitants to one another.

"Until midnight," says Felix to Emma. Emma blushes.

What would you have done in her place, Madame my reader? Shh!

IV. The First Night

Young people of twenty, whose burning imagination decorates with the most cheerful colors the frightful vice of seduction, read the last chapter of this story; you will see there the punishment that the wrath of Heaven reserves for the individual without honor who has sworn the loss of innocence; perverse men that society welcomes and too often honors, take a frightful example therefrom, striking for your imagination, and avoid the society of those whose crimes you might be meditating; and you whose senses want to make you criminal, think about Felix.

"She loves me, I'm sure of it; her eyes and her weakness have shown me clearly enough. Well, if I possess her tenderness, do I not have some right to her favors? Not without marriage...marriage might come later, and anyway, have I not read in ten philosophical works that marriage is nothing but a vain formality, instituted by superstition and politics? Have I not read that natural union is the only reasonable one? And if ten great writers have traced those reflections, it is because they have profoundly analyzed sage verities. They have reflected for me; I shall act for them."

Such is the insensate discourse that Felix concludes as he emerges from his bedroom an hour after having gone into it.

Midnight
The north wind launches itself turbulently through the obscure corridors of the château; the quivers of the twelfth stroke of the hour of murders fade away as they are prolonged beneath the vaults of that ancient swelling.

Felix, burning with desires and full of hopes, advances rapidly toward his victim's room; his hand touches the door of the sanctuary of innocence. Sacred refuge of modesty, you are no longer a barrier to halt the steps of the audacious.

Felix is next to the bed; a difficult slumber agitates the defenseless beauty, a fatal obscurity surrounds the young man; a long sigh is heard. Unfortunate child! Shame and dishonor are threatening you, and perhaps a pleasant dream is surrounding you with the most gracious illusions.

Felix, Felix, have remorse! You are only twenty years old...your heart is still pure...you are scarcely a man; yes, I know, a frightful presentiment is agitating you, you are not unaware that you are about to commit a crime.

Quarter past midnight.

Flee, then! You approach the door...good, cross the threshold, and you remain virtuous... You're coming back! Wretch! What demon is pushing you toward that bed? For mercy's sake, flee it, it is your doom, and that of innocence, that you're meditating...

It is all over; she is lost; the culpable lover lifts the last veil of modesty, he precipitates himself upon the young woman; the burning fever of lust redoubles his strength; he sticks his lips to those of the beauty he adores, and whom he is about to soil with his deadly amour...

Proud of his triumph Felix gets up again; frightful cries strike his ear.

"My brother...come and avenge me!"

It is his sister.

The unfortunate fellow! The darkness and his passion have deceived him as to his victim. Agitated by horror and fear, he regains his bedroom; a pistol presents itself to his sight...he ceases to live...

Three months after that event, the French Revolution bursts forth in all its force. The Marquis de Lavo emigrates with his daughter, and Felix's unfortunate sister follows her father and mother to the scaffold.

PEDRIGO; or, HIS FATHER'S SON

I. The Two Colics

"Quietly then, Señor," said Rosa to young Pedrigo, introducing him at midnight, stealthily, into the house of her mistress, the charming Isabelle, niece of the Alcalde of Valladolid. "Quietly, if you please, Señor, my master is a light sleeper, almost anything wakes him; and his late wife, of whom he was as jealous as a tiger—or rather, a Spaniard—was never able to able to make the top of his face swell, so much was he on his guard, night and day."

"Here's what reassures fearful soubrettes, which corrupts honest judges, delivers from the claws of the Inquisition and emerges from the pockets of monks to pass to their mistresses; here, in sum," Pedrigo replied to Rosa, giving her a few gold coins, "is what would obtain the hand of my charming Isabelle, if her uncle were not a fool, and if I only had a father as noble as Philip V."

During that conversation, Pedrigo and his pretty guide had arrived at the door of Isabelle's bedroom; Rosa opens the door; the affectionate Spaniard is at his beauty's bedside; the Alcalde's niece wakes up; Pedrigo stifles the first cry of fright with a kiss, and the charming Isabelle, entirely reassured, does not even have the strength to scold her lover for having corrupted Rosa, Rosa for having allowed herself to be corrupted, or Pedro for having come into her bedroom by night, and what is worse, for having dared to kiss her.

Do you recall, my dear reader, the first kiss that you deposited on the rose-colored lips of your mistress? Do you remember, with as much joy as me, the incendiary effect that that little devil of a kiss produced? Have you forgotten the sweet confidence that was established between you and your beauty? If you profited from it you have done well; if you neglected the instant of abandonment it caused, I beg your pardon, but you are an idiot.

But Monsieur Author, you are abusing your advantages, and your words are much too brisk for me, whom no one has treated thus in the forty years I've existed...

Oh, I get it, my dear reader; your anger proves to me that you missed the charming opportunity that I mentioned just now. Well, Monsieur, it's not with indecision that one brings great enterprises to a conclusion.

When Alexander, of glorious memory, said to himself: "I shall be the greatest monarch in the world," he assembled his troops, departed, fought, and came back victorious.

When in the nineteenth century, a certain Cicero of my acquaintance finds, between two digestions, a luminous thought to express, astonished by the activity of his imagination, without reflecting on what he is going to say, for fear of forgetting it, he advances heavily toward the throne of eloquence, appears there, makes people laugh, and goes to sit down thinking about the truffles of his next dinner...

When my procurator had decided on Monday to take a wife, he found her on Thursday, married her on Saturday and was cuckolded on Sunday.

That is the way that all great hearts act; that is how you ought to have acted yourself; that is the way that Pedrigo...

"Never, Señor," I shall never let you do that," said Isabelle, pushing her lover away. "I saw you a fortnight ago, while out walking; you pleased me; I loved you; we told one another so; that's all very well, but my uncle has promised my hand...I am in despair, but you shall not enjoy the rights of a husband without having received the title..."

She speaks like an angel, that little Isabelle; I already love her with all my heart.

Pedrigo, who as unconvinced by all the good arguments of his mistress, had lifted the veils that revealed to him the secret charms of her beauty, and would doubtless have profited from his advantages in spite of the efforts that were opposed to his own if Rosa, hurtling no the room, had not terminated his amorous combat.

"Save yourself, Señor Cavalier, "save yourself," cries the obliging Rosa as she enters, "Señor the Alcalde has one of his colics; on descending from the throne he might well make a nocturnal round, and you'll be caught. Great God! I can hear him coming..."

"Me too," replies Pedrigo. "I would kill your Alcalde if I didn't want to make him my uncle."

As he concludes that sentimental speech he opens the window, clings on externally to the bars of a shutter, and waits, half-undressed, lodged on a window-sill like a flower-pot, for what it pleases Heaven and the Alcalde to order as to his fate.

Rosa closes the window, and the Don enters his niece's room, holding his belly and making the most comical grimaces.

"Oof! Aiiee! My God, what pain, truly, I'm dying...."

"May Heaven wish it," mutters the soubrette.

"Are you ill, Uncle?" Isabelle asks him, drawing her bed-curtain.

"I'm in agony, my niece. The bed redoubles my agony, and I'll spend the night in this armchair, next to your fireside, in order to be nearer to..."

"What an idea!" cries Rosa "Does Señor want to die...?"

"Eh! But Mademoiselle," says the Alcalde, putting on his spectacles to decide he usage of a petition that he removes from his pocket as a precaution, "tell me how, at this hour of the night, I find you up and dressed as if you haven't been to bed...? Oh, Heaven, it's getting worse, I can't stand it anymore, I have to go..."

And an officious colic had spared the young woman a response that it would have been embarrassing to make.

While the Alcalde was punished for his gluttony, Isabelle recovered from her disturbance and Rosa was dying of fear, another scene had taken place in the street under the windows of the Don's house. A patrol—for in Valladolid there are patrols, as there are in Paris, to protect honest people and punish rogues; which does not prevent the rogues from robbing the honest people and sometimes doing worse than that—a patrol as valiant as all those of our worthy National Guard was passing tranquilly by when the leader of those noble warriors took it into his head to look at the clouds, with the intention, if it looked like rain, of abridging the circuit of his men in order to protect a brand new uniform that brought out his fifty-year-old graces marvelously. Now, because, when there is an intermediary object between Heaven

196

and earth, it is impossible not to see it, he saw the tail of Pedrigo's shirt, which a zephyr was agitating gently above the heads of the soldiers.

"Friends," cried their chief, "what is that standard? Does Señor the Alcalde want to change our national colors, or is the yellow fever rife in his house? There's a question of a marriage in the family; no one will be at the wedding if that's the case..."

"I have it, Señors," says one of the worthies of the cohort, trembling. "It's a rallying signal, certain proof of a revolution, a plot or a conspiracy, of which the Don must be a part."

"But, loyal defenders of the fatherland," replies the leader, looking at his men with a victorious expression, "if the Alcalde is conspiring, who the devil wants to denounce the Alcalde?"

An embarrassing situation! How could the frightened minds of our Spaniards have inspired a response? In truth, I don't know, and I scarcely care, but there was now another subject of astonishment for our interesting patrol.

"Comrades," the commandant continues, excitedly, "The Señor's flag seems to me to be covering a rather particular form."

If this adventure had happened in Paris, any National Guard apothecary would have been able to recognize the object in question, but in Valladolid everyone sticks to his métier, and a worthy merchant is not obliged to expose himself to rheumatisms, gout and nocturnal powders under pain of quitting his boutique to go and visit the hall of discipline.

A ray of blonde Phoebe had just discovered the posterior forms of Pedrigo to the astonished eyes of the soldiers; cries immediately departed from all their mouths.

"It's a man!" they repeated, in unison. "It's a man!"

Spaniards in Valladolid are clever; they had divined his sex, having only seen his posterior...

The unfortunate Pedrigo, trembling and terrified, paler than the moon that had served him so poorly, saw that he was between two dangers, the patrol on one side, and the Alcalde in the bedroom of his mistress on the other.

Nature came to his aid; while the warriors, eyes staring and mouths open, were considering their prey, suspended between Heaven and Earth, a frightful detonation was heard, a humid mixture of heterogeneous elements fell on the nonplussed troop and covered it with the results of Pedrigo's panic. Fear had operated on the unfortunate lover as gluttony had on the Don's entrails; the soldiers fled precipitately.

Pedrigo took advantage of that to let himself slide down into the street along the shutters of the entresol and the ground floor. Rosa saw his fall, uttered a scream, and before the members of the patrol had recovered from their astonishment, he was already at home.

From that day on, those soldiers were in bad odor in Valladolid.

II. Rosa

Pedrigo lived in an outlying district of Valladolid, and the Alcalde lived in the city center. Now, one hour to reach his lodgings, one hour to wash himself, perfume himself and one hour of sleep makes three hours, if I can count—which is not certain, given that I was taught by a bailiff who had become a monk as a result of failed speculations, or false speculations, during which he had contracted the habit of counting as double that which was single and as triple that which was double, and although an old proverb says that wolves do not eat one another, men of law, who resemble them somewhat, nevertheless denounce their colleagues, and would have infallibly sent him to the galleys if the friar's hood and wide-sleeved robe had not offered him a salutary protection.

Pedrigo had therefore been asleep for sixty minutes when his bell woke him up, caused him to open his door, and put in his arms the lovely Rosa, nonplussed by the promptitude of the young man.

"But Señor, it's frightful to treat a poor girl thus who has come to see you to serve her mistress; you're making me repent of my step."

"Well, just one quick kiss."

"There..."

"Then another...."

Then a beautiful brand new gold coin, which went to keep company in the girl's pocket with the duros that Pedrigo had given her during the night.

"Now, my dear child, let's chat."

And so saying, he sits her down on his bed, places himself beside her and asks her what he can do for her.

"I've come, Señor Cavalier," Rosa replies, still blushing with a residue of pleasure, "on the part of Isabelle, to ask you three questions. The first is, what is your name? The second is, what is your estate? Then I have to ask you what you count on doing in order to become the husband of my mistress."

"I count on doing," Pedrigo replies, "what turtledoves do in the month of May, sensible women sometimes, and young lovers all the time. My dear Isabelle wants to know my name; here it is: Don Pedrigo, son of his father; my estate: idler."

And with that, he kisses her…for the third time.

"Oh, that's too much!" says Rosa, pushing him away. "I want to be able to give my mistress a satisfactory response, and what you're charging her to tell me will certainly doom you in her mind."

"Does the lovable Isabelle share the ridiculous notions of her uncle?" says Pedrigo, sharply. "In order to marry her, does one have to be noble, like the King? In that case, I can't pretend to her hand, since the only nobility I have is that of my heart, and my sentiments..."

"I'm convinced," replied Rosa, "but after all, what is your family?"

"Oh, I understand, my beautiful child, "it's my story that you want to know. Well, listen; it isn't long. Nineteen years ago, at eleven o'clock in the evening, it was pitch dark, which is quite natural; an old woman named Laura, an inhabitant of this city, was sitting next to her hearth watching her olla boil when three blows loudly struck on her door gave her such a fright that she tipped her supper over and ran to the extremity of her cabin, expecting at any moment to see the Devil, a frightful phantom, or some other terrible monster come into her home. Nothing did, though. Reassured, after an hour or so, she opened her door, and found outside a little basket containing a beautiful child—that was me—and a letter whose contents read:

"I have been unfaithful to my wife; she would have me stabbed if she knew; Pedrigo is the fruit of my amours; I confide him to the good Laura, and will never see my son again as long as I live.

"To that letter was adjoined an enormous sum of money, contained in a purse and a wallet. Laura took me, kissed me, nourished me with the milk of her goat, and put me in school when I was old enough to go. Three months ago, I came out, because of the death of my protectress; she left me the residue of her treasure, and I am at present a bachelor, fortunate in the love of Isabelle, grateful for the kindness of her chambermaid and calling myself the son of my father, since I cannot name myself otherwise."

"That's all well and good, Señor Pedrigo; but, in spite of your love for Isabelle, your gratitude for me and your fortune, which, like you, seems to have fallen from the sky, and finally, in spite of all the surprising things you've just told me, remember my prediction well: you won't marry my mistress; you won't be the nephew of an Alcalde and the master of your very humble servant Rosa, if you don't present yourself at the Señor's house two days hence with a father richer, more powerful and nobler than the Marquis of San Carlos, first class grandee, possessor of an annual income of three million , and furthermore, the future nephew of the Alcalde of Valladolid, the uncle of Doña Isabelle. It's to that gentleman that the hand of my dear mistress is promised; she weeps over it, thinking of you."

"I'll console her, my dear Rosa."

"Oh, no matter what a man you are for consolations, be sure that you'll only administer any to Isabelle after a good marriage made before..."

"But that's what I intend..."

"Wait for the end of my sentence," says the soubrette, "...a good marriage made before the judges of Valladolid."

"In that case, lovable Rosa, I'll spend half my fortune on horses, carriages, livery, etc. Then I'll present myself to the Alcalde as the King's prime minister, I'll marry my beauty in twenty-four hours, and once I'm her husband, I'll resume my name of Pedrigo and continue to seek my father, but without fatiguing myself, for I have no need of him, thanks to his magnificent presents."

"If you can't find anything better than that to steal Isabelle from the first-class grandee," the servant responds, "you'll be a bachelor for a long time. Look Señor Pedrigo, your amiable, frank and generous manners have seduced me; I'm entirely at your service."

"In that case, my friend, permit me to prove my gratitude to you."

"It's not worth the trouble, Monsieur."

"What do you mean, trouble? It's a pleasure, Rosa, and a very keen pleasure, my child."

Oh Heaven! Monsieur...you're stifling me! My dear Franciscan...my good monk..."

"Eh?" says Pedrigo, bursting out laughing, "What is she saying? My dear Rosa, you're mistaken, I'm not a monk."

"Eh? Who mentioned monks?" says Rosa.

"You, my child—you have a very short memory."

"Me, Monsieur Pedrigo, I named a monk? Oh yes, a Franciscan brother...he's a friend of the Alcalde, a reverend brother, a respectable man, full of kindness for me...I was appealing to him for help, to prevent you from embracing me so forcefully."

"Good, child, very god—I believe everything you say...but tell me then, what you want to do for my service?"

"This, Señor Pedrigo. At seven o'clock this evening, an old woman covered by her mantilla will approach you on the promenade and give you a sign to follow her, and guide you by a roundabout route to a place where I shall be with your Isabelle. There, we can agree together the means of enabling her to avoid marrying the Marquis of San Carlos. But above all, promise me to be more reasonable than last night."

"Naughty girl," says Pedrigo, "you're making fun of me. No matter; I forgive you because I'm desperate. Be tranquil, I'll be good, faith of a man in love...."

With that, Rosa leaves, and Pedro gets dressed. We shall see in the next chapter whether he keeps his trousers on for long.

III. Which Will Surprise the Reader

There is between Spanish promenades and French promenades a difference as sensible as that between a coquette and a devotee, a brilliant ball in the Chaussée d'Antin and a certain salon in the Rue Saint-Louis—in sum, everything that is absolutely contrary. In Paris, the women pretend to lower their eyes or turn their head when someone looks at them; in Spain, when night begins to fall, the ladies and demoiselles, whom no cavalier ever accompanies, spread out in the public places; there, winks, nudges and nods of every species are given with the most voluptuous intentions. The lover loses himself in the crowd, and finds himself next to the woman who loves him; mercenary duennas deploy an immoral activity in all directions; in sum, what one hides with the greatest care in France is advertised in Spain with the greatest immodesty, and some woman of high society who is received everywhere, as soon as she finds a stranger to her liking in the square, entices him, invites him to follow her, and a rich present given by the beauty is often the vile recompense of a moment of brutality. Each country to its own; it's all right by them, and by me too; the population gains by it, and the list of affected husbands doesn't lose.

Seven o'clock chimed in the sixty-four convents of Valladolid, for in Valladolid one sees a great many monks—which is to say, a great many libertines, hypocrites and rascals who live on the dupes they make, and whose income was once inscribed in the great book of the Inquisition's murders. Pedrigo, as light as Zephyr and as handsome as Ganymede—who, between us, was a rather dirty fellow—disposed to run the gallant adventure that was to hasten his happiness, left his house to go to the promenade where he was to meet the officious old woman, but he had scarcely taken a few steps when a woman, her face hidden by her mantilla, named him as she passed close by and invited him with a gesture to follow her.

"Let's go," said the child of his father. "Rosa, thinking of my fatigues this morning, had charged her duenna to save me half the route; I'll be grateful for her attention; a pretty woman always finds with me a recompense to match the service."

Pedrigo's guide, after having traversed several deserted streets, stopped in front of a little door, knocked on it three times, indicated it to the young man when it opened, and fled at top speed.

Reader, who has fallen asleep over the *Thousand-and-One Nights*, the novels of Miss Radcliffe and a host of other interesting and soporific works, in which you have seen little doors, mysterious old women, treasons, brigands, sepulchers, phantoms, palaces and thatched cottages, have you ever found privies? No, I'll wager. Well, that is, however, to what my duenna led Pedrigo, who, in the darkness, without any suspicion of the dirty trick that was apparently being played on him, had arrived next to a certain conduit from which repulsive miasmas had immediately driven him back.

Surprised by that strange boudoir, my hero disposes himself to regain the door; he pushes it, presses the catches: vain efforts; it had locked of its own accord, in such a way that it is impossible to open it again.

"Pardon me, Monsieur Author, for interrupting your story; I only have one question to ask you; I'm not Monsieur M*** des Deux SS*, to whom no one takes the trouble to respond, although he speaks to everybody, so you can chat with me for a moment. Do you believe, my friend that the bizarre is wit? Do you believe that extravagance is originality?"

My dear reader, your questions bear a very close resemblance to impertinences. No matter, I shall have the generosity to satisfy you by telling you that something you do not understand at present might perhaps by explained to you by the subsequent paragraph, and that just as indecision is harmful in certain cases, so too great a precipitation is dangerous in some others. So, when you are jealous of your wife, look at her twice before beating her; when you want to speak in a public place about the color of a coat or the form of a hat, reflect on the consequences of your speech before saying anything; finally, when you read a book, finish it before judging it.

Pedrigo does not know whether to be amused or annoyed at the bad joke of which he is the victim; his fortunate character, however, triumphs over his ill humor, and a loud burst of laughter causes an unfamiliar sound to resonate from the vaults of his comical prison, habituated to other outbursts.

At the same time, a little door opens alongside him, and a young woman dressed in white, as pretty as all the Amours, invites him to accompany her. Pedrigo obeys without being begged, and follows his guide for quite a long time along a narrow corridor that terminated in a little staircase. He goes up the stairs, and finds himself, after a few minutes, in a beautiful bedroom, in the middle of which is a table, elegantly laid.

"Who is that meal for?" the young man asks.

"For you and me," replies the unknown woman.

"Oh!" exclaims Pedrigo. "I'm not in Isabelle's house, then?"

"I don't know her," the young woman tells him, "but I know you as the most amiable cavalier in Valladolid, and its under that title that I wanted to receive you. I beg your pardon for having you enter via the place where I found you; it's a precaution I take in order to leave my servants in ignorance as to my conduct, in my husband's absence."

"All right," says Pedrigo. "Sine that's the way it is, I pardon you with all my heart, but have the goodness to render me my liberty, for I didn't think that I was coming to your home in following your duenna, and I have business elsewhere this evening..."

"It's frightful to treat poor Julia thus," replies the beauty, sobbing. "She isn't accustomed to such insults.

Personally, I have never been able to see a woman weep without being moved; Pedrigo was the same, so he was moved to such an extent that, after having embraced Julia, he sits down beside her and starts to sup with a hearty appetite.

Poor Isabel, Heaven will avenge you!

Gradually, little by little, Julia's pins were ejected,[13] along with the pins of the fabric they attached, and no

---

[13] This wordplay does not translate; the French *épingle* [pin] is used metaphorically in a phrase that means to make much of something, so, so the phrase can be read to imply that Julia is calming down as the cause of her distress is removed.

charm had quit its place along with the pins that attached the fabric, which was furiously different from the attire of certain Parisian beauties of my acquaintance...

When one has removed all the thorns from a rose, what does one do with the flower? One breathes in its scent; one savors it. Pedrigo was disposing himself to scent, to savor...when Julia, uttering a slight cry, fainted, or pretended to faint.

Frightened by that accident, Pedrigo took the young woman in his arms, carried her to her bed, and lavished a thousand urgent cares upon her...

I do not know by what prodigy the lights were spontaneously extinguished, but I am assured that the most perfect obscurity suddenly reigned in the room, and Pedrigo moved away from the bed swiftly in order to discover the cause of that event. Julia, having come round, called him back, claiming that the clumsiness of her servants was the natural cause. He came back immediately and found, astonishingly, that his lady's charms had disappeared with the light, during his brief absence. Why was that? How was it? You will learn as quickly as he did.

A faithful historian, need I tell you that the boiling Pedrigo allowed himself to be carried away by his youth and the seduction of the moment; that the room was immediately illuminated again; that the curtains of the bed opened violently; and that Pedrigo, wanting to give Julia one last kiss, encountered beneath his lips the bald and decrepit forehead of a horrible old woman, whose brazen visage was ornamented by a thick layers of carmine...?

The traveler bitten by a frightful reptile and the hunter pursued by a ferocious tiger do not draw away with any more promptitude from the object of their terror that Pedrigo from his dowager's bed. And if he had one wish at that moment it was to be able to make the bedroom walls recoil, in order to avoid even the sight of that tender beauty.

"Oh, la la la!" she said to him, laughing. "Did you think you were the first handsome lad to testify amity to me? Know, my friend, that the most beautiful youth of Valladolid has occupied your place. I'm immensely rich; I like the conversation of ardent young men, and I've made the conquest of all those in the city by means of the stratagem by which you were duped. None has boasted about it; that's quite simple, and you'll do the same. Now you're free to leave, and to go to your Isabelle. Good night, my friend, I salute you."

As she finished speaking she dropped behind the bed and disappeared. The little door opened, and Pedrigo fled, cursing perfidious young women, nocturnal adventures, amorous old coquettes and the accursed supper for which he had just paid such an expensive bill.

IV. The Second Night

Pedrigo ran to the street where Isabelle lived; he saw the blinds lowered; the house seemed to have been abandoned. A sad presentiment immediately took possession of his soul; somber thoughts agitated him.

One of the Alcalde's neighbors told him that since midday, the hour at which a very important individual from Madrid had arrived at the house, Isabelle, her uncle, Rosa and the newcomer had departed in the latter's carriages for the Alcalde's country house.

That habitation was situated two leagues from Valladolid. The clock of the nearby church is chiming nine times. On a good horse, Pedrigo can be with his beauty in an hour. He does not hesitate to set forth. His courser seconds his impatience. He has arrived...

Gentle melancholy, demi-mourning of the heart, lent my style your enticing charm, give it your dolorous grace. You, inspiring angel of Goethe and Delille,[14] if there are a few roses in my story, cover them, like theirs, with the crepe of sadness,

A vast garden surrounded the Alcalde's house. Pedro descends from his horse, approaches a door fitted into a high wall, sees it open, to his great astonishment, and finds himself in the company of the pretty Rosa.

"My duenna told you about our prompt departure, then?" she says

"I didn't see her, my dear Rosa, but it doesn't matter; here I am. Can I talk to my charming Isabelle?"

"Alas, Señor Pedrigo, I only have one hope any longer to render you her husband, and I fear that it will not be realized, The Marquis of San Carlos arrived at the Alcalde's house this morning; as everything had been agreed in advance for his marriage to your friend, there was talk of concluding it immediately; it's tomorrow that it will take place, in this vicinity. The Marquis, a widower and very old, desires it thus in order to avoid the splendor and noise of a fête. Why, Señor Pedrigo, what's the matter?"

Rose could have talked to him for a full hour without obtaining any more response. The cruel news that she had just announced to him had caused him to feel all his love for Isabelle. Leaning against a weeping willow,

---

[14] The reference is to the poet Jacques Delille (1738-1813), the particular work the author has in mind is probably *La Pitié* (1802), reflecting on his ruination by the Revolution.

his head in his hands, he seemed to have lost the sentiment of life.

That dolorous scene passed in an arbor in the garden into which Rosa had just led the unfortunate lover.

Suddenly, a frightful storm commences; the thunder, with a frightful din, threatens to destroy the world; the bellowing waters that border the Alcalde's vast park mingle their dull groans with the terrible noise of the thunderbolts. Intermittently, pale lightning-flashes display the ravages of the frightful tempest; hail destroys the hopes of the cultivators, and water and fire seem to have joined forces to add to the horror of the spectacle.

Midnight

"There's no more happiness, for me, then!" cries the unfortunate Pedrigo. "I must renounce the hand of the only woman who has made me know love, and because unjust fate has only given me a common name on earth, without a title, without nobility, I see myself precipitated into the depths of an abyss of dolors by an individual more favored than me by fortune. Barbarous prejudices of ranks and dignities, I abhor you as much as I have always despised you!"

Moderate yourself, Señor," says Rosa, frightened by his cries. "I'm lost if anyone catches us."

"What do I see?" says Pedro. "Who is advancing toward us through the foliage?"

"The unhappy Isabelle," responds the Alcalde's niece, weeping.

"Isabelle, dear Isabelle! I see you once again…oh, forgive me, I beg you, my insensate transports of last night; I was only considering you then as a charming woman; now I adore you as the most perfect thing there is in the world! Oh, for pity's sake, swear to me never to be the wife of San Carlos; I protest that I will not survive your frightful marriage..."

Clad in a long white dress, which, soaked by the storm, designed her enchanting figure, Isabelle seemed to be the angel of peace weeping over the world's misfortunes.

"Señora," Rosa said to her, "an effort of courage might yet save you. Elope! The danger that you would be running in staying here excuses your step. The Alcalde is forcing you to endure the Marquis; remove yourself from his power; tomorrow you will be the wife of your lover, and the malevolence of men, disarmed by your virtues, will forget the fault to which you owe your happiness."

"Worthy Rosa," says Pedrigo, "that advice, dictated for my felicity, merits you my eternal gratitude. Dear Isabelle, come with me, I implore you; in a few hours, nothing will disunite us; one moment of resolution, and you are free—let's elope!"

And Isabelle's beautiful hand is in his; he covers it with caresses, and draws the young woman away in spite of her resistance.

One o'clock.

"Stop, vile seducer! Infamous kidnapper!" cries the Marquis of San Carlos, hurling himself at the young man, sword in hand.

"So this is the cause of your long absence," says the Alcalde to his niece, choking with fury.

Pedrigo, depositing Isabelle in Rosa's arms, receives a wound in the breast before arming himself. Immediately retreating a few steps, he opposes a vigorous resistance to the Marquis, but, seeing that the other wants to kill him, he profits from the advantages that his strength gives him over the old man, and his murderous weapon soon strikes his enemy in the heart and lays him down on the grass, wet with his blood.

"Pedrigo, what have you done" cries Rosa.

"Pedrigo!" repeats the Marquis. "What name do I hear? Young man, who is the author of your days?"

"Abandoned child," replies Isabelle's lover, sadly, throwing away his sword. "I never knew him..."

"Oh, ultimate horror!" say the old Marquis, raising himself up. "Wretch! You are your father's murderer!"

"My father..."

"Alas, yes; it's me that a perfidious valet has deprived until now of your presence, by fleeing, after having stolen from me, without telling me what he had done with you... You were found on the fourth of January nineteen years ago..."

"My father, my dear father,"

"My son, my Pedrigo; widowed of my first wife, I would have recognized you, and made your happiness, and it's your parricide that has given me death..."

"Don't finish, I beg you," says the unfortunate son. "Help, please, help..."

And Pedrigo, lying on the grass, red with the Marquis' blood, applies his discolored lips to the horrible wound that he has inflicted on his father, and, amid the most tender embraces, sees the poor fellow expire in his arms.

Lightning strikes at that moment; in a horrible delirium Pedro draws away rapidly from San Carlos' cadaver. The profound waters that bathe the Alcalde's garden offer him both a prompt death and forgetfulness of his crime. He does not hesitate...and disappears forever from the bank.

Isabelle buried her dolors and her beauty in an austere convent, and perished subsequently in a fire during the last Spanish Wars.

THE COTTAGE IN ZURICH

I. The Dinner

"Eat, then, my nephew."

"But Uncle, I'm not hungry."

"Ah, that desolates me. If you looked at yourself in your mirror you'd be astonished by the change in your features. You were young, robust, with a rosy complexion, three months ago when I came to settle here in Pars after my return from the islands and I took you out of school in order to have you with me. Now you're no more than skin and bone. And what has caused it? Amour, I'll wager. Damn it, Monsieur, I've been amorous too in my time, but never in a fashion as stupid as yours. Come on, Gustave do as I do and you'll be fine.

"Listen, in my voyages overseas, I sometimes remained for six months between the sky and the water, without even seeing the shadow of a skirt. When I finally touched land I began by seeing all my merchandise unloaded; then I stored it all in the warehouse; then I drank two bowls of punch, and afterwards I thought about tenderness; I courted my beauty in a quarter of an hour—and the proof that I made love better than you is that there probably isn't a port in the ocean where I haven't left regrets...and children. Well, you definitely don't want any dinner?"

"No, my dear uncle."

"Damn it, Gustave, I'm going to get angry; I love you like the son I lost, and whose place you've taken, but if you don't swallow that chicken wing and that glass of wine, I'll disinherit you."

And Gustave, seeing his uncle's chagrin, eats, or makes a semblance of eating, in order to satisfy him.

"Jacques!" shouts Captain du Lusse to his valet. "Clear the table and give me my pipe."

"Here it is, Master."

Snap! It is broken by an angry movement of the old mariner.

"Come on, cabin boy, another."

"Captain," Jacques replies, "here's a dozen. If you break them all like the first, I'll go in search of others."

"I believe, damn it, that that rogue is trying to preach me a lesson," cries du Lusse. "I'd have you tied to the yardarm, scoundrel, if we were still at sea."

Jacques, hearing the storm rumble, runs downstairs. Encountering Mademoiselle Julie, the cook's daughter, on his way, who is bringing up the captain's dessert, he pushes her in front of him.

The young woman, in saving herself, pushes the door of her room; Jacques pushes Mademoiselle Julie, who does not push anything, but allows herself to be pushed; while pushing the demoiselle, Jacques collides violently with a pot, which is not a pot of flowers, and breaks it. The old cook comes running at the noise, and Jacques' backside and her daughter's cheeks attest for a long time after the event that Gothon upholds the honor of her family.

For his part, Gustave, frightened by his uncle's fury, was getting ready to go out when the captain stopped him, made sure that the door of his drawing room was closed, and threw himself at his nephew's knees, weeping like a child.

The surprised young man lifts him up and begs him, while hugging him in his arms, to let him know the cause of his dolor.

"Of my dolor?" replies the mariner. "Don't you know, ingrate? For two months I've been imploring you to tell me why you've lost your appetite, your color and your gaiety, but you persist obstinately in keeping your cruel secret."

"I could tell you, my dear uncle, that I'd be afflicting you needlessly by opening my heart to you, but no matter, I'll tell you everything; I owe that mark of tenderness to your affection for me..."

"Two months ago I was introduced into the house of Milord Doldbridge..."

"Oh yes!" says the captain, interrupting. "That Englishman so renowned for his phlegm and his eccentricity: spleen personified."

"Himself," Gustave continues. "I saw his daughter, the adorable Miss Amanda; to chat with her once and adore her for the rest of my life was the work of a moment; I dared not confess my sentiments to her..."

"And you were wrong," the captain puts in, again. "Me, I only told a beauty that I loved her after having proved it to her. Anyway, what did your miss do?"

"She accepted my homages, Uncle. I wrote to her; after the most ardent insistences, she promised to respond, but the person she entrusted with her letter betrayed her by taking it to her father."

At this point, the old mariner delivers such a shock to the tea table that he tips it over in the middle of the drawing room; then, without saying a word, he makes a sign to the nonplussed Gustave to continue.

"Milord," the young man does on "immediately forbade his house to me, and since that fatal day, I haven't even had the hope that you might be able to obtain my Amanda's hand for me..."

"Eh! Why is that, if you please, my nephew? I have an income of eighty thousand livres; I'll give it all to you, and I'll only ask your Englishman, in exchange for my fortune, for one little girl for you to amuse yourself by making her a wife; damn it, milord would be very stupid to refuse the bargain."

"Uncle," says Gustave, "Amanda's father possesses six or seven millions, and his daughter will only marry, I'm sure, a man as rich as she is..."

"Bah! Bah! I'll go to see the fellow," says the captain, "and if it's only necessary, to have as much money as him, to go into commerce, well, damn it, I'll go."

As he concludes this discourse, which depicts all the generosity of his heart, the dear uncle puts on his hat, and tries in vain to open the door, which Jacques, as he ran away, has locked.

In a thunderous voice he calls for the cabin boy. At that moment, however, Jacques is fleeing the vigorous foot of Julie's mother.

"Jacques! Tom! Plumb!" cries the furious mariner.

They are in the tavern; for the present, Bacchus is their only master.

What does our man do? Searing like a damned soul, he opens one of the drawing room windows, which overlooks the courtyard; a cart full of forage is beneath; he says adieu to Gustave and launches himself on to the hay; his nephew, having not had time to retain him, sees him descend softly between the bundles in the cart.

Scarcely is he in the courtyard than he breaks his cane over the shoulders of the first valet he encounters, throws the debris in his face and heads at a run for the house of Milord Doldbridge.

We shall see what he does there.

II. The Duel

"Where is Monsieur going?"

No response.

"Who is Monsieur seeking?"

No response.

"What does Monsieur want?"

Without listening to Milord's concierge, the captain continues striding toward the vestibule of the house. A Swiss can be a frank beast, a machine with a rifle, when a sovereign has bought him, or an automaton started by pulling a string when a great lord has soiled him with his livery, but in spite of his well-known nullity, the Helvetian possesses one quality rare in our century, which is his fidelity—so the Englishman's Cerberus, paid to prevent bad lots, thieves and madmen from entering his master's house, hastened to run after the mariner and question him.

"Monsieur is doubtless going to see Milord?"

"Yes."

"But Monsieur is not wearing a black coat."

"So what?"

"Milord only receives people in that costume."

"May the sea engulf you, rogue, with your costume. I have a coat, waistcoat and trousers, you can see that I'm not in my shirtsleeves. Go on, get out of the way, or I'll treat you as a corsair."

And the captain, furious at the resistance that the Swiss is opposing to him, seizes the compatriot of William Tell with a vigorous arm, and sends him to reflect at the back of the courtyard on the vivacity of French mariners, who have over their neighbors in Great Britain the advantage of being as good soldiers on land as at sea.

Captain du Lusse arrived at Milord's apartment at the moment when the most stupid and least gallant—in a word, the most English—custom had sent away at the end to dinner the fair sex who ornament it so well.

In France, when the champagne has sparkled in our glasses, all vain ceremonial is forgotten; it is the moment of the meal when wit is deployed, when the conversation becomes animated, when clever remarks are made, when the new play is praised and torn apart, the beloved artiste raised to the clouds; it is during the quarter of an hour when the Cyprus and Alicante wines tease or avid palates agreeably that reputations in society commence or finish...

"The Chevalier de Floris," an antique Baronne affirms, "is really a man of merit; he dances like Paul, rides a horse like Franconi and also has all the amiability of the old court, giving his arm with such grace..."

"Which costs the good lady dear," whispers the young Comtesse de B**** in the ear of a future vice-consul. "The Baronne gives the Chevalier a thousand écus a month to have him at her orders very day."

"And all night," responds the young man, to pay his court to his malicious neighbor.

With that, the pretty conversationalist deploys her fan to hide a non-existent blush.

"What is the new play?" asks a jealous old litterateur of an equally envious colleague, whistled as often as he is. "A rhapsody, made after three plays on the same subject, a bad work, in which the most respectable doctrines are mocked, and such plays succeed, which my latest comedy can't be finished; it's a horror, the century's taste has been lost."

At the other end of the table a young law student and the pretty Amélie, a mischievous fifteen-year-old, are taking advantage of the noise that is being made around them to talk in low voices about certain little matters that interest them...

In sum, in our country, dessert is the moment of the most amiable joy, but the pleasure is not complete if beauty does not participate in it.

Miss Doldbridge and her friends, therefore, had retired to the drawing room when the old mariner penetrated into Milord's dining room, after having distributed forceful blows of his fists to the domestics who attempted to prevent him from entering.

Once arrived there, his wrath having calmed down, du Lusse is about to speak to Lord Doldbridge, whom he has recognized, when all the valets, having been rallied, enter simultaneously behind him. One seizes him by the legs, three others by the shoulders, and they all prepare to carry him away.

The furious captain gathers his forces, frees one of his legs, kicking the dining table, and tips it upside-down, along with all the tipsy lords, whom the shock has caused to lose their equilibrium.

The captain, having succeeded in ridding himself of his aggressors, runs to Lord Doldbridge, seizes him by the collar, and, using him as a shield, opposes him to the redoubled blows that the valets want to rain down upon him.

Suddenly, a luminous thought occurs to him; without letting go of Milord's collar, he pushes him in front of him against a door, which cedes to his effort, immediately turns round and makes him close it with his backside, as he had opened it. Then, after having sat him down in a convenient armchair, he asks him to forgive his abruptness, tells him the reason for his visit, and is getting ready to speak to him at length when the lord, without saying a word in response, gets up, runs to his writing-desk, seizes two pistols, with which he arms himself, and, taking the captain's hand, takes him down into his garden by way of a little hidden stairway that gives access to the room where they were.

Having arrived in a covered pathway, Lord Doldbridge hands one of his weapons to the mariner, and makes the following speech:

"Monsieur, I've known you by name for a long time; your nephew has offended me by writing to my daughter; but you have insulted me even more by the indecent conduct that you have just manifested in my home. The door of the room in which we were just now will soon be broken down; I have left open the one that leads to this place, and when people arrive here they will find one of us lying dead. Take aim and fire."

The captain, who sees at that moment Amanda lost to Gustave forever, attempts to put a few objections to the Englishman.

"Fire," says Doldbridge, "or you're a coward."

At that word, du Lusse takes aim at the Englishman, and the two weapons discharge simultaneously.

The captain is intact; Amanda's father falls.

III. The Disappearance of a Milord

"This way, this way, dogs of valets," shouts the captain, running toward the house. "Milord is dead. I've killed Milord, go help him quickly; vinegar, a sling, eau de Cologne, surgeons, old linen."

Amanda had scarcely heard the sound of the gun-shots when, heading in the direction from which the sound had come, she met the captain, who was running toward the house as she was coming out.

"Follow me, Mademoiselle!" he cries to her. "You are the cause of your father's death."

At that cruel speech, the young woman falls in a faint at du Lusse's feet. The latter, without thinking of helping her, snatches away the shawl that is covering her pretty shoulders, makes bandages of it, returns to his Englishman, looks at him, shakes him, perceives that he only has a broken arm, from which the blood is flowing abundantly, and is getting ready to staunch it when Amanda's companions, who are looking for her in the garden, arrive at the place where Lord Doldbridge is lying, and, struck with terror at the sight of him, all fall backwards on to the grass, one after another.

The captain redoubles his cries, and is soon surrounded by all the domestics of the house; while some of them hasten around Milord and the ladies, others take possession of the Captain, calling him a murderer.

Du Lusse, for the first time in his life, controls himself; he keeps silent, while roaring with fury, and meditates a means of getting away from his guards; because, he thinks, privately, an offended man can give a beating to the rogue who insults him; if he has several aggressors and in his self-defense he breaks a few teeth, blackens a few eyes and splits a few chins, the spectators laugh at the expense of the beaten, applauding the victor; but wounding his adversary grievously in a duel without witnesses to depose as to the equality of the combat, becomes too dangerous for him run any risks, and...

The captain would doubtless have reflected on many other fine things if Milord's bandaging had lasted longer, but the bleeding had just been stopped and two strong lackeys had loaded the wounded man on to their shoulders. Amanda, having emerged from her faint, was holding her father's hand, marching alongside the porters and the captain, contained by six Englishmen. The cortege was terminated by the troop of ladies who had only had nervous fits for the time necessary to render them interesting and to establish a small reputation in society for sensibility, for which a pretty woman in always ambitions.

In the meantime, what were the milords doing whom we left in the Doldbridge dining room, some on top of the table and others underneath it? They were asleep in the debris of the feast, in the state in which our good patriarch Noah showed his backside to his son.

Milord was put to bed; his friends were sobered up by pouring a carafe of cold water over each of their heads; the misses, the wives and the mistresses hastily took possession of their hats and shawls, and discretion put everyone out of the door.

The captain would have liked to put himself there too, but his six guardians did not let go of him, in spite of Amanda's insistence that they allow Gustave's uncle to depart. Finally, Lord Doldbidge, making an effort, told his daughter what had happened, and ordered that du Lusse be set free, whom he heaped with apologies in dismissing him. The Captain, without responding to him, bowed, turned his back on him, and left. He was still resentful at having been arrested like a murderer...

Damn, damn and double damn, he said to himself, as he returned home. *Was it necessary for me, who has only ever seen Englishmen at cannon-range to find myself with those pirates for more than two hours, and not to have done anything yet about what took me to the home of that eccentric Doldbridge? Triple salvo, my nephew; when you send me to visit such people again I'll be as dry as the biscuit after two years of voyaging. Let's go, my decision is made; I'll send my Gustave round the world, that will distract him; I haven't spared my trouble to obtain his beauty for him; I've conducted myself as a good uncle, but I had a contrary wind. Too bad, I can't expose myself to any more squalls...*

"Well, my dear uncle, for what should I hope? Who have you seen? What have you done for my happiness?" cries the young man, on seeing the mariner, who has just come in.

"What have I done, my nephew? Pull up that chair and listen. First of all, I jumped out of the window in order to get outside more rapidly. I've lacerated the buttocks of a Swiss by throwing him on his backside from end of a courtyard to the other; I've beaten ten or twelve of Milord's lackeys, who wanted to stop me getting to him. I've laid out fifteen fat Englishmen under their dinner table; I've made use of Doldbridge's shoulders like Bayard's breastplate to spare myself the blows that his valets were landing on me. Finally, I fought a duel with him because he told me that you'd offended him by writing to his daughter...and the dear papa is now in his bed, with a broken arm, and a good lesson that I've given him..."

"Oh, Heaven!" says Gustave. "Uncle, you've doomed me. Lord Doldbridge will never consent to my happiness; you've raised an eternal barrier between Amanda and me."

"By Sainte-Barbe," replies du Lusse, angrily, "that's a fine recompense for all that I've done for you. Go away, Gustave, you're an ingrate, I detest you..."

"Of, forgive me," says Gustave, "my chagrin cause me to misunderstand tour generosity momentarily, but I'll never forget it..."

Bang bang! Someone knocks on the drawing room door.

"Come in!" shouts the mariner. "Oh, it's you, Jacques, gallows-bird, rogue, drunkard, corsair, enraged Turk who locks me in and exposes me to breaking my neck on the cobblestones of my courtyard. What do you want?"

"Captain," replies the cabin boy, "it's a letter..."

"Hand it over. That's all right, go away, and remember that if you do anything stupid again, I'll blow out your brains at the first opportunity. Here, Gustave, open this letter and read it to me. Who's it from?"

"Lord Doldbridge," the nephew replies.

"The Englishman again! Does he want a revenge? Go on, read."

"*Monsieur le Capitaine, by the time you receive my note I will have quit my house, in order to remove my Amanda forever from your nephew's pursuits; do not take any steps to discover my residence, they will be futile. Console your relative for the loss of my daughter, and believe that I am your servant, Lord Doldbridge.*"

It would be impossible to depict Gustave's despair in reading that letter.

Without losing any time, his uncle summons his valets, pays their wages, only keeping Jacques, orders him to pack the trunks and to order post horses for the following morning at five o'clock. He informs his nephew of the resolution he has made to make him travel.

Gustave, plunged in his dolor, scarcely hears what his uncle says. The captain smokes a pipe, drinks a glass of punch and goes to bed.

As soon as Gustave sees his uncle go out he envelops himself in his cloak and heads for the Englishman's house. Everything is calm around it; he goes into the street, knocks on the door; he is told that Milord disappeared two hours ago, that it is believed that he left by the garden door with his daughter, and that his house is to be put up for sale the next day.

The young man withdraws and goes home, with despair in his heart.

IV. Six Months in Ten Minutes

If I were writing a novel I would be very embarrassed at this moment; to reach the catastrophe that will finish my story, I far that too great a rapidity in the march of my events might tax plausibility, and might remove from them in consequence the charm of verity that every sensate reader loves to encounter in the works he peruses. But here, as a narrator of real facts, I shall present them as they occurred, and will not be responsible for the conduct of my history, since Clio is the only muse I have invoked in commencing them.

"Let's go, coquin, into the saddle," the captain cries to the postillion who is to conduct him to the first staging-post; I'll pay double, rogue, but let's get out of this bitch of a city, where I should never have set foot.

"Well, Gustave, talk to me then. Oh, good God, what is it? Stop, dog, rogue, bumpkin, stop your nags, Gustave is ill. Hey, Monsieur Café-owner, orange-flower, lemonade, fresh water, everything you have, but hurry…"

And the captain, increasingly alarmed by the state of the young man, who has fainted by his side while sitting next to him in the post-chaise, leaps out of the carriage and collides head on with the café-owner, who is emerging from his shop with his hands full of everything the dear uncle had ordered.

The collision was so violent that the merchant dropped everything he was carrying, and du Lusse, immediately perceiving that his nephew had suddenly emerged from his faint, threw some money at the proprietor of the occiput against which he had damaged the projecting part of his face, and, blocking his nose with his handkerchief in order to stem the abundant flow of blood, he climbed back into the carriage, after having sent Jacques to the coachman's seat with a kick up the backside, about which the cabin boy, accustomed to his master's mischief, said nothing, and thought no more.

With that, the vehicle set off again, and the three individuals it contained traveled, in six months, through France, Germany and Italy. We shall not follow our voyagers in their various courses; we shall limit ourselves to saying that in every country to which they went, Gustave was profoundly sad, that no pleasure, however stimulating or varied it might be, could extract him from the somber melancholy that the loss of his Amanda had caused him. We will add that the mariner, desolate at this nephew's chagrin, treated Jacques a little more abruptly, and that Jacques, sometimes forgetting the obedience and subordination that he owed his master, had a few canes broken over his shoulders and deducted from his monthly wages, as expenses made in his regard.

In the sixth month of their voyage, our little company was retained for few days, by a slight indisposition on Gustave's part, in an inn in the city of Zurich in Switzerland. In the evening of the day before their departure from France the captain went into his nephew's room and enquired as to the state of is health with an anxiety that was only too visible to Gustave. The latter, surprised by the disturbance and disorder evident in his uncle's speech, begged him to inform him of the cause of his agitation.

"Damn it," cries du Lusse, "if I were dealing with a young man more courageous than you, I'd reveal without hesitation the sad secret that has been weighing on my heart for several hours, but I dread your fiery head and your sensible soul too much to inform you of it."

Acting thus was not wise politics on the mariner's part, for to speak in that way was to excite the unhappy young man's curiosity to the highest degree. But du Lusse had never inhabited Courts, and the perfidious art of deceiving his fellows and stabbing them while caressing them was unknown to him.

"I beg you, Uncle, to tell me what you want to keep from me," Gustave replies. "The cruel ignorance in which you're leaving me will be even more frightful than anything you could tell me."

"Oh, if I thought that...," cries the captain, "But after all, why should I hide it from you? It's a misfortune, a very great misfortune, undoubtedly, but by Saint Nicolas, it was bound to happen sooner or later; besides which, the event doesn't change your position at all, you'll be neither happier nor more mournful, and then..."

"Oh, for mercy's sake, tell me immediately what it is, my dear uncle."

"Well, my friend, my dear nephew, my good Gustave, know that Amanda..."

"Amanda, Uncle! What's happened to her?"

"She is no more," du Lusse continues. "In consequence of a malady of chagrin, she has ceased to live."

"And I still exist...," were the only words that the unfortunate Gustave pronounced.

"One of my friends, who know Lord Doldbridge, has just written to inform me of the catastrophic event," the mariner continued. "The poor child died on her arrival in London."

Du Lusse expected that news to produce a terrible effect on his nephew, so he was astonished not to hear him relieving his woe in horrible imprecations against Heaven and earth, oaths, blasphemies and other locutions for the particular use of worthy men of his own species. He did not know that great dolors are mute, and that the bleak and silent state of Gustave was more to be dreaded on his behalf than fury or tears. The worthy mariner therefore mistook for calm what was actually the extremity of despair, and went to bed, after having placed Jacques as an exterior sentinel at the door of his nephew's room.

Scarcely does the young man find himself alone than he leaps out of bed, dresses in haste, writes a few words of eternal adieu to his uncle, and is preparing to go out when, all of a sudden, Jacques, faithful to his orders, stops him and informs him of the express instruction he has received to oppose his departure in the case that the desire takes him to go out.

"Listen," Gustave replies to the cabin boy, "you're not happy with my uncle; come with me. I'm not going out to commit suicide, but to go and bury myself in some profound, unknown retreat, where dolor will terminate my life."

And Gustave, deceiving the poor fellow, gives no thought to the fact that his death will deliver the unfortunate he trying to corrupt to all the horrors of poverty. Jacques, who cherishes the young man, takes his cloak and some savings, and follows him in silence, promising himself to inform the captain as soon as possible of his nephew's retreat. Thus, two people who believed themselves to be sure of one another, both deceived one another.

Thus men in general play with the good faith of their fellows. Thus, Monsieur de *** marries for convenience Mademoiselle de **, swearing to love her uniquely, but she has a lover, he keeps his mistress, and so on, and so on, and so on...

V. The Third Night

O night, chaste goddess of silence and repose, it is you that I invoke! The scene that I have to depict has need of your somber colors.

Divine muse of the eloquent Young, cause to pass into my lines a few of the thoughts that flowed from his dolorous pen to be engraved in letters of fire in tender and melancholy souls!

All was calm in the fortunate plains of that happy part of Helvetia; the earth, fatigued by the toil of the active laborer, was aspiring in long draughts the gentle dew of darkness. Balm and wild thyme perfumed the atmosphere with their delightful odors, and the vast fields of Switzerland, whose horizon the darkness hid from the eyes, presented to the imagination of the traveler the intoxicating image of a boundless, sublime, unlimited liberty, like that the fortunate fatherland of Gesner[15] once enjoyed.

Eleven o'clock.

But what do I hear, two leagues from the city of Zurich? What sound suddenly comes to trouble the reverie of the unfortunate Gustave and extract from his apa-

---

[15] The Swiss naturalist Conrad Gessner (1516-1565).

thetic lethargy the man who is accompanying him, and whom the young man has not yet been able to send away?

Oh Heaven! They are the cries of a mother, a tearful mother; she runs from the depths of a wild valley and throws herself at the feet of du Lusse's nephew and his companion, embracing their knees.

Messieurs," she says, "oh, Messieurs, save him, save my son! Alas, perhaps it's too late and my child is lost to me forever; help, in the name of God, help; don't resist my tear, they're those of a mother. Save him, save my son..."

"Woman," relies Gustave, lifting hr up, "what is the cause of your tears? Where is the danger that threatens you?"

Without responding, the peasant woman seizes the young man's arm and drags him after her.

"I saw him," she says, "heading toward my home as I was about to go to sleep; our peasants have been searching for him for some time; dolor and dread have troubled my mind; my husband is away, for a week I've been alone in my cottage. I feared that the monster might break down the door, which lacks solidity, and I went out through a window overlooking my garden in order to seek help from my neighbors, when I saw you. Alas, I didn't bring my child for fear that cries might accompany his awakening, and that the rabid man, attracted by the sound, might fall upon him and upon me."

She approaches her dwelling as she finishes speaking. "Oh Heaven!" cries the unhappy mother. "Look, look...I'm not mistaken, my cabin is open, the monster is inside. Great God! There he is, bending over my son's cradle! Earth, swallow me!"

With those words, the woeful mother falls in a faint on her threshold.

Midnight

A ray of the night star penetrates into the cottage, and as he goes in, Gustave sees a man leaning over the little cradle, in which the whiteness of the linen is soiled with atrocious bloodstains. The noise he makes on going into the humble abode seems to extract the terrible man from the contemplation of his innocent victim. He turns toward the travelers; at that moment the moon disappears; a profound darkness surrounds the actors of the horrible scene...

Jacques perceives Gustave's danger instantly; he precipitates himself toward the unfortunate who is so redoubtable to approach and, lowering his head rapidly to avoid being bitten, seizes him around the body, knocks him down, and taking advantage of the fact that he is stunned by the fall, throws over him one of the mattresses from the poor woman's bed. Then, invoking his master's aid, they employ their combined efforts to deprive the victim of his noxious breath.

Horrible moans, muffled by the frightful torture, pierce Gustave's heart; trembling and dazed, he withdraws his knee precipitately from the breast of the unfortunate he is stifling, one last effort of whom pushes the torturer away.

"I'm dead!" is the only word that precedes his death...

And, his nerves contracting, shoving aside the mattress that hides the fact, Gustave reveals to his eyes the adored features of Amanda, illuminated by a faint light escaping from the rustic hearth.

"What do I see?" the unfortunate lover cries, shivering. "What frightful vision is alarming my senses? Is it not you, dear love, that a cruel demon is offering to my gazes?" he says, launching himself upon the inanimate body of the celestial girl. He drags her to the hearth, reanimates with his breath a few coals ready to burn out, and convinces himself of his terrible misfortune by their expiring glow...

I am dropping the pen...

Gustave is mad...

Whatever it costs me to return to facts so sad, I owe an explanation of some of them.

The news of Amanda's death had been invented by the captain, with the aim of curing his nephew forever of his amour. Instructed by a messenger that Jacques sent regarding Gustave's condition, he came to fetch him from the valley, and devoted the rest of his life to caring for him, in expiation of his life, the primary case of the last woes of the unfortunate young man.

Wanting to know why Miss Amanda had forsaken the garments of her sex and how she came to be in Switzerland, the captain learned that Lord Doldbridge was traveling with his daughter in the locale, that the young woman, informed by the owner of an inn where they had stayed that Gustave was a few leagues away, had wanted to join him, and after having procured male attire, had fled from her father's home; but, bitten in the vicinity of Zurich by a rabid dog that was laying waste to the region, she had become herself the most frightful among the most terrible.

SF & FANTASY

Adolphe Alhaiza. *Cybele*

Alphonse Allais. *The Adventures of Captain Cap*

Henri Allorge. *The Great Cataclysm*

Guy d'Armen. *Doc Ardan: The City of Gold and Lepers; The Troglodytes of Mount Everest/The Giants of Black Lake; The Abominable Snowman*

G.-J. Arnaud. *The Ice Company*

André Arnyvelde. *The Ark; The Mutilated Bacchus*

Charles Asselineau. *The Double Life*

Henri Austruy. *The Eupantophone; The Olotelepan; The Petitpaon Era*

Barillet-Lagargousse. *The Final War*

Barbot de Villeneuve.*The Naiads/Beauty & The Beast*

Cyprien Bérard. *The Vampire Lord Ruthwen*

S. Henry Berthoud. *Martyrs of Science; The Angel Asrael*

Aloysius Bertrand. *Gaspard de la Nuit*

Richard Bessière. *The Gardens of the Apocalypse; The Masters of Silence*

Chevalier de Béthune. *The World of Mercury*

Albert Bleunard. *Ever Smaller*

Félix Bodin. *The Novel of the Future*

Pierre Boitard. *Journey to the Sun*

Louis Boussenard. *Monsieur Synthesis*

Alphonse Brown. *City of Glass; The Conquest of the Air*

Émile Calvet. *In a Thousand Years*

André Caroff. *The Terror of Madame Atomos; Miss Atomos; The Return of Madame Atomos; The Mistake of Madame Atomos; The Monsters of Madame Atomos; The Revenge of Madame Atomos; The Resurrection of Madame Atomos; The Mark of Madame Atomos; The Spheres of Madame Atomos; The Wrath of Madame Atomos* (w/M. & Sylvie Stéphan)

Jean Carrère. *The End of Atlantis*

Félicien Champsaur. *Homo-Deus; The Human Arrow; Nora, The Ape-Woman; Ouha, King of the Apes; Pharaoh's Wife*

Didier de Chousy. *Ignis*

Jules Clarétie. *Obsession*

Jacques Collin de Plancy. *Voyage to the Center of the Earth*

Michel Corday. *The Eternal Flame; The Lynx* (w/André Couvreur)
André Couvreur. *Caresco, Superman; The Exploits of Professor Tornada* (3 vols.); *The Necessary Evil*
Gaston Danville. *The Perfume of Lust*
Camille Debans. *The Misfortunes of John Bull*
Captain Danrit. *Undersea Odyssey*
C. I. Defontenay. *Star (Psi Cassiopeia)*
Charles Derennes. *The People of the Pole*
Georges Dodds (anthologist). *The Missing Link*
Charles Dodeman. *The Silent Bomb*
Harry Dickson. *The Heir of Dracula; Harry Dickson vs. The Spider*
Jules Dornay. *Lord Ruthven Begins*
Alfred Driou. *The Adventures of a Parisian Aeronaut*
Odette Dulac. *The War of the Sexes*
Alexandre Dumas. *The Return of Lord Ruthven; The Man who Married a Mermaid* (w/P. Lacroix)
Renée Dunan. *Baal; The Ultimate Pleasure*
J.-C. Dunyach. *The Night Orchid; The Thieves of Silence*
Henri Duvernois. *The Man Who Found Himself*
Achille Eyraud. *Voyage to Venus*
Henri Falk. *The Age of Lead*
Paul Féval. *Anne of the Isles; Knightshade; Revenants; Vampire City; The Vampire Countess; The Wandering Jew's Daughter*
Paul Féval, *fils. Felifax, the Tiger-Man*
Charles de Fieux. *Lamékis*
Fernand Fleuret. *Jim Click*
Charles-Marie Flor O'Squarr. *Phantoms*
Louis Forest. *Someone is Stealing Children in Paris*
Arnould Galopin. *Doctor Omega; Doctor Omega and the Shadowmen* (anthology)
Judith Gautier. *Isoline and the Serpent-Flower*
H. Gayar. *The Marvelous Adventures of Serge Myrandhal on Mars*
Louis Geoffroy. *The Apocryphal Napoleon*
G.L. Gick. *Harry Dickson and the Werewolf of Rutherford Grange*
Raoul Gineste. *The Second Life of Doctor Albin*
Delphine de Girardin. *Balzac's Cane*
Léon Gozlan. *The Vampire of the Val-de-Grâce*
Jules Gros. *The Fossil Man*
Jimmy Guieu. *The Polarian-Denebian War* (2 vols.)
Edmond Haraucourt. *Daah, the First Human; Illusions of Immortality*
Nathalie Henneberg. *The Green Gods*

Eugène Hennebert. *The Enchanted City*

Jules Hoche. *The Maker of Men and His Formula*

V. Hugo, P. Foucher & P. Meurice. *The Hunchback of Notre-Dame*

Romain d'Huissier. *Hexagon: Dark Matter*

Jules Janin. *The Magnetized Corpse*

Gustave Kahn. *The Tale of Gold and Silence*

Gérard Klein. *The Mote in Time's Eye*

Fernand Kolney. *Love in 5000 Years*

Paul Lacroix. *Danse Macabre; The Man who Married a Mermaid* (w/Alexandre Dumas)

Louis-Guillaume de La Follie. *The Unpretentious Philosopher*

Jean de La Hire. *The Fiery Wheel; Enter the Nyctalope; The Nyctalope on Mars; The Nyctalope vs. Lucifer; The Nyctalope Steps In; Night of the Nyctalope; Return of the Nyctalope*

Etienne-Léon de Lamothe-Langon. *The Virgin Vampire*

André Laurie. *Spiridon*

Gabriel de Lautrec. *The Vengeance of the Oval Portrait*

Alain le Drimeur. *The Future City*

Georges Le Faure & Henri de Graffigny. *The Extraordinary Adventures of a Russian Scientist Across the Solar System* (2 vols.)

Gustave Le Rouge. *The Dominion of the World* (w/Gustave Guitton) (4 vols.); *The Mysterious Doctor Cornelius* (3 vols.); *The Vampires of Mars*

Jules Lermina. *The Battle of Strasbourg; Mysteryville; Panic in Paris; The Secret of Zippelius; To-Ho and the Gold Destroyers*

Maurice Level. *The Gates of Hell*

André Lichtenberger. *The Centaurs; The Children of the Crab*

Maurice Limat. *Mephista*

Listonai. *The Philosophical Voyager*

Jean-Marc & Randy Lofficier. *Edgar Allan Poe on Mars; The Katrina Protocol; Pacifica 1, 2; Robonocchio; Return of the Nyctalope;* (anthologists) *Tales of the Shadowmen 1-13; The Vampire Almanac* (2 vols.)

Ch. Lomon & P.-B. Gheuzi. *The Last Days of Atlantis*

Camille Mauclair. *The Virgin Orient*

Xavier Mauméjean. *The League of Heroes*

Joseph Méry. *The Tower of Destiny*

Hippolyte Mettais. *Paris Before the Deluge; The Year 5865*

Louise Michel. *The Human Microbes; The New World*

Tony Moilin. *Paris in the Year 2000*

Michael Moorcock's *Legends of the Multiverse*

José Moselli. *Illa's End*
John-Antoine Nau. *Enemy Force*
Marie Nizet. *Captain Vampire*
Charles Nodier. *Trilby and The Crumb Fairy*
C. Nodier, A. Beraud & Toussaint-Merle. *Frankenstein*
Henri de Parville. *An Inhabitant of the Planet Mars*
Gaston de Pawlowski. *Journey to the Land of the 4th Dimension*
Georges Pellerin. *The World in 2000 Years*
Ernest Pérochon. *The Frenetic People*
Pierre Pelot. *The Child Who Walked on the Sky*
Jean Petithuguenin. *An International Mission to the Moon*
J. Polidori, C. Nodier, E. Scribe. *Lord Ruthven the Vampire*
P.-A. Ponson du Terrail. *The Immortal Woman; The Vampire and the Devil's Son; The Police Agent*
Georges Price. *The Missing Men of the* Sirius
René Pujol. *The Chimerical Quest*
Edgar Quinet. *Ahasuerus; The Enchanter Merlin*
Jean Rameau. *Arrival; in the Stars*
Henri de Régnier. *A Surfeit of Mirrors*
Maurice Renard. *The Blue Peril; Doctor Lerne; The Doctored Man; A Man Among the Microbes; The Master of Light*
Restif de la Bretonne. *The Discovery of the Austral Continent by a Flying Man; Posthumous Correspondence* (3 vols.); *The Fay Ouroucoucou* (2 vols.)
Jean Richepin. *The Crazy Corner; The Wing*
Albert Robida. *The Adventures of Saturnin Farandoul; Chalet in the Sky; The Clock of the Centuries; The Electric Life; The Engineer Von Satanas*
J.-H. Rosny Aîné. *Helgvor of the Blue River; The Givreuse Enigma; The Mysterious Force; The Navigators of Space; Vamireh; The World of the Variants; The Young Vampire*
Marcel Rouff. *Journey to the Inverted World*
Marie-Anne de Roumier-Robert. *The Voyage of Lord Seaton to the Seven Planets*
Léonie Rouzade. *The World Turned Upside Down*
Han Ryner. *The Human Ant; The Superhumans*
Louis-Claude de Saint-Martin. *The Crocodile*
Frank Schildiner. *The Quest of Frankenstein; The Triumph of Frankenstein*
Nicolas Ségur. *The Human Paradise*
Pierre de Selenes: *An Unknown World*

Norbert Sevestre. *Sâr Dubnotal: Vs. Jack the Ripper; The Astral Trail*

Angelo de Sorr. *The Vampires of London*

Brian Stableford. *The Empire of the Necromancers (1. The Shadow of Frankenstein; 2. Frankenstein and the Vampire Countess; 3. Frankenstein in London); The Wayward Muse; Eurydice's Lament; The Mirror of Dionysius; The New Faust at the Tragicomique; Sherlock Holmes and The Vampires of Eternity; The Stones of Camelot* (anthologist) *News from the Moon; The Germans on Venus; The Supreme Progress; The World Above the World; Nemoville; Investigations of the Future; The Conqueror of Death; The Revolt of the Machines; The Man With the Blue Face; The Aerial Valley; The New Moon; The Nickel Man; On the Brink of the World's End; The Mirror of Present Events; The Humanisphere*

Jacques Spitz. *The Eye of Purgatory*

Kurt Steiner. *Ortog*

Eugène Thébault. *Radio-Terror*

C.-F. Tiphaigne de La Roche. *Amilec*

Simon Tyssot de Patot. *The Strange Voyages of Jacques Massé and Pierre de Mésange*

Louis Ulbach. *Prince Bonifacio*

Théo Varlet. *The Castaways of Eros; The Golden Rock.; The Martian Epic* (w/Octave Joncquel); *Timeslip Troopers* (w/André Blandin); *The Xenobiotic Invasion*

Pierre Véron. *The Merchants of Health*

Paul Vibert. *The Mysterious Fluid*

Villiers de l'Isle-Adam. *The Scaffold; The Vampire Soul*

Gaston de Wailly. *The Murderer of the World*

Philippe Ward. *Artahe; Manhattan Ghost* (w/Mickael Laguerre); *The Song of Montségur* (w/Sylvie Miller)

Victor Margueritte. *The Bacheloress; The Companion; The Couple*